I'd been looking forward to this football course for ages, and it was so like my evil half-sister to do something to ruin it, and on my birthday too. Especially when I was already worrying about having to confess my secret to Mum and Dad...

For my dad, who took me to my very first football match

www.thebeautifulgamebooks.co.uk

ORCHARD BOOKS
338 Euston Road, London NW1 3BH
Orchard Books Australia
Level 17/207 Kent Street, Sydney, NSW 2000

First published in 2009 by Orchard Books

ISBN 978 1 40830 421 1

Text © Narinder Dhami 2009

A CIP catalogue record for this book is available from the British Library.

10 9 8 7 6 5 4 3 2 1

Printed in Great Britain

Orchard Books is a division of Hachette Children's Books, an Hachette UK company.

www.hachette.co.uk

THE BEAUTIFUL GAME

Friends and football – the perfect match

HANNAH'S SECRET

NARINDER DHAMI

ORCHARD BOOKS

PROLOGUE

Hannah realised that this was her chance. If only she was brave enough to take it...

Keeping out of sight in the shadows at the top of the stairs, she peered down into the hall. Her dad had just stormed out of the kitchen, yelling at the top of his voice.

'The answer is NO, Louise!' he shouted. Then he'd left the house, banging the front door behind him. A moment later, Hannah had heard her mum come out of the kitchen, go into the study and slam that door shut too.

Hannah's heart was beating like crazy. Her mum

and dad hardly ever argued, but this was different. This was *huge*. And Hannah knew exactly what they were arguing about because just a moment or two before, she'd had her ear pressed to the kitchen door, listening. She'd only run upstairs in a panic when she'd thought she was about to be discovered.

Hannah tiptoed down the stairs. She knew she shouldn't be doing this, but she couldn't help herself. And if her dad ever found out... Hannah gulped. She didn't want to think about *that*.

It took Hannah only a few moments to discover that the Christmas card she was looking for, the one that had caused the argument, wasn't displayed with the others in the Fleetwoods' large living room. She stood there uncertainly for a moment, next to the Christmas tree decorated with silver and blue baubles. What had her dad done with the card? Hannah wondered. Maybe he'd taken it with him.

But then she had an idea.

On edge, her heart in her mouth, Hannah glided silently past the study door and into the kitchen. She flipped up the lid of the bin and there, pushed down almost out of sight under used teabags and damp, crumpled squares of kitchen towel, she found what she was looking for. A Christmas card with a picture of a white cat draped in red tinsel on the front. The card was torn into small pieces.

Hannah's hands trembled uncontrollably as she fitted the card back together like a jigsaw. Her mind was racing. Now that she had this information, what was she going to do with it? Could she *really* find the courage to betray her family like this?

Or maybe it wasn't really a betrayal at all, Hannah thought. Maybe this was finally a chance to take control of her life...

CHAPTER ONE

'Here comes the birthday girl!'

I had just reached the bottom of the stairs when the kitchen door was suddenly flung open from inside, and I almost jumped out of my skin. My mum and dad stood there in the doorway, grinning all over their faces.

'Happy birthday!' they yelled, blowing party whistles in my direction. They were more excited than I was. Behind them I could see that the kitchen had been decorated with balloons and streamers and a banner had been hung across the conservatory doors. *Happy birthday, Hannah!*

'Thanks,' I yawned. I had still been half-asleep when I stumbled downstairs, but I was waking up fast. I'll warn you now, my mum and dad are *always* over the top. But that's kind of fun for birthdays and Christmas. It's not quite so much fun at other times.

'My little girl is twelve today!' Dad announced. He escorted me ceremoniously over to the kitchen table and sat me down in front of a large pile of presents wrapped in gold paper with pink silk ribbons and bows. 'I feel so old.'

'You *are* old, Dad,' I replied with a grin. 'Can I open my presents now?'

Mum and Dad gathered round me, excited as little kids, as I unwrapped the first parcel.

'Come on, Hannah,' Dad said impatiently, as I neatly removed the tape, bit by bit, and opened up each end. 'Just rip the paper off!'

'Oh, she's always been the same, hasn't she?' Mum sighed. 'Remember when she was little, it used to take her all of Christmas Day to open her presents.' She sniffed and bit her lip. 'I can't believe where all the years have gone…'

'Mum!' I groaned. 'Don't start crying on my birthday, *please.*'

I opened up the square parcel. I thought I knew

what it was, and I was dead excited. I'd wanted the slim, glossy, pink mobile phone I'd seen in a magazine for *ages*.

It was the same phone, but it wasn't pink. It was an upgrade of the model I'd asked for, but it was metallic grey. I stared down at it, deliberately allowing my long brown hair to fall over my face to hide my disappointment.

'I know you wanted the pink one, honey,' Mum rushed to explain, 'but your dad checked them out, and he thought this one was better value. It has more features for the money.'

That figures. Dad always knows best.

'I love it.' I shook back my hair and smiled. I'm used to hiding what I'm really feeling. I do it all the time.

Don't take this the wrong way, I love my mum and dad to bits. But it's easier to go along with my dad all the time, like Mum does, rather than make a stand.

Or maybe I'm just a coward.

'And now this one!' Dad took the next present from the pile and handed it to me with a flourish. I could see instantly from its size and shape that it was a DVD. I'd asked for several football ones, including *Arsenal's Glory, Glory Years* and *The History of the FIFA World Cup*. I wouldn't have been too disappointed with Keira Knightley's latest film either.

Carefully I took the wrapping paper apart, ignoring Dad's loud sighs of mock-impatience. Then I blinked several times when I saw what was inside.

It was a DVD all right, but like the phone, it wasn't what I was expecting. There was a photo of me on the cover, and I was wearing my team's football strip. The picture had been taken from the sidelines at one of our games. A few weeks ago I'd joined Springhill Stars Under-Thirteens Girls' team, and we wear purple kit. It was unfortunate that my face in the photo was bright red, which didn't look at all stylish combined with my purple shirt as I went charging across the pitch. I was gritting my teeth and grimacing, my hair was a mess and flying all over the place. It was possibly the worst, most unflattering photo of anyone ever taken anywhere in the civilised world.

Things did not improve when I saw the title of the DVD.

'*Hannah Fleetwood, Future Captain of the England Women's Football Team,*' I read aloud.

Mum and Dad were roaring with laughter and patting themselves on the back, looking totally smug.

'Isn't it great, Hannah?' Mum said, almost bursting with pride. 'It was all your dad's idea.'

'I'll bet,' I said weakly.

Dad grabbed the DVD from me and ran over to the TV on the dresser.

'You'll love this, Hannie,' he said, slotting the disk into the machine. 'I know you're starting that intensive football training course today, but if you watch this every week, it'll help your game no end.'

I thought I could guess what was coming next, and, sadly, I was right. A picture of me running with the ball flashed up on the TV screen. I could tell that it had been filmed when we played St Barton Under-Thirteens just after I'd first joined the team a few weeks ago. We'd lost 2-1.

Dad turned the volume up. I winced as his voice came from the TV, loud and clear.

'Come *on*, Hannah! You have to use your brain in football, not just your feet – *think* about your next pass. See the whole picture, don't just try and get rid of the ball as fast as possible!'

Dad and Mum come to all my matches. Mum films me at every game, while Dad stands on the touchline, shouting instructions at me. They did it for four years when I was playing for Lightwater Girls, and they carried on doing exactly the same thing when I moved to Springhill Stars. Now they've made a DVD. *Great.*

I stared at the TV. I remembered this bit of the game perfectly, and I didn't need a film to remind me. Flustered by Dad yelling, I panicked and lost my head and the ball at the same time. There were loud groans on the DVD soundtrack from my parents, and loud groans in the kitchen too.

The next clip was from our match against Seventrees, when I gave away a penalty and we lost 3-2. I cringed as I saw myself tackle the opposition's striker clumsily just inside the box. She collapsed dramatically in a heap, clutching her leg.

'*Hannah*!' Dad shouted from the touchline. Mum had actually taken the camera off me for once, and instead had filmed Dad dancing up and down in frustration like Rumpelstiltskin in an Arsenal shirt while the other parents looked on in amazement. 'What have I *told* you about making a tackle? Timing is *vital*! Never take your eye off the ball!'

'We've included lots of stuff from this season,' Dad explained proudly. 'Not just from your new team, but from when you were playing for Lightwater too—'

I couldn't stand it any longer.

'Thanks, Dad, that's brilliant.' I forced a grateful smile as I grabbed the remote control and stopped the DVD. 'I'll watch the whole thing later.'

Gloomily I wondered just how *many* of my mistakes Dad had decided to include in the film. *Would there be any of the good bits?* Because, although you might not think so, I am, actually, not a bad player at all. I got into the Springhill Stars first team, no problem, even though I was the new kid on the block.

'Good idea,' Dad agreed. 'You should probably watch it every day. Maybe show it to your new team too.'

I gulped. *No way.* I'd become a Spurs supporter first.

'You obviously all need some extra coaching,' Dad went on. 'It's really disappointing that you've got no chance of making the play-offs.' He frowned. 'I should have checked the team out a bit more before we signed you up. Apparently they finished mid-table last year too. Maybe we'll think about a move for next season—'

'Dad!' I muttered sulkily, 'I'm not moving teams *again*!' I'd had to leave Lightwater Under-Thirteens and all my mates behind because a few months ago we'd moved house, right over to the other side of town, to be nearer to my new school. 'And anyway, the team *did* get to the semi-final of the County Cup.'

I longed to defend our fantastic coach, Freya Reynolds, whom we all idolised, but I knew from experience that there was no point. Dad had made his mind up, and that was that.

'Yes, but remember what I always say.' Dad stared hard at me, his brown eyes serious, and I sighed under my breath.

'*Winners don't come second*,' I mumbled. I had heard this several million times ever since I started playing football years ago.

'Or third or fourth.' Dad nodded with satisfaction. 'No one remembers the semi-finalists in a cup competition, only the winners.'

I didn't reply. I guess that Dad's right, in a way. But *everyone* can't be a winner every time, can they?

'That's what our coach always said when I had my trial at Chelsea,' Dad went on. 'Winning is everything.'

I tried to look interested, but it was difficult. Like I said, I've heard this millions of times before. Dad had a trial at Chelsea when he was a teenager years ago, and no one is allowed to forget it. He decided not to become a professional footballer in the end, and he went to university to study engineering instead. He started his own business and now he and Mum run it together and it's really successful. But Dad still works out and keeps himself fit, and he thinks he knows as much about football as a professional does.

I opened my other presents and I got everything I'd asked for, like new jeans and a black denim jacket and a whole heap of make-up, as well as some lovely gifts that I wasn't expecting. But somehow, after seeing that DVD, a little of the magic had gone out of my day.

'Right, time for your birthday breakfast, darling,' Mum said when I had opened the last little box and found silver earrings with a pair of tiny football boots hanging off each one.

'Oh, Mum, *no-o-o*-!' I wailed. My mum's breakfasts are legendary throughout the land. She has a waffle-maker, a French-toast maker, a hi-tech chrome juicer which looks like an instrument of torture and every other type of breakfast gadget you can think of. 'I don't want much. I'm going to be running around a football pitch in an hour or two.'

Freya Reynolds had nominated me and five other girls from our team to attend an intensive training course for the first week of the Easter holidays. It was being held at the ground of our local professional club, Melfield United, and I was *so* looking forward to it. For one thing, Mum and Dad would not be there, capturing all my mistakes on film and yelling at me. I could just enjoy my football, for once.

On the other hand, I was a little nervous of spending so much time with the other five girls from my team. I didn't know them very well, really. Although three of them went to the same secondary school as me, Greenwood High School, I wasn't in any of the same classes. Freya was really keen for us to all get to know each other better, though – she'd kept going on about how important it was to build up a bond with our team-mates, especially as me and one of the other girls, Katy, were complete newbies. Freya had got us all to swap mobile numbers last week, and she'd urged us to spend as much time as possible together and to observe each other's play closely during the course.

'What time are Chloe and Danni coming over for your birthday sleepover tonight?' Mum asked, slipping her *World's Best Mum* apron over her curly blonde hair.

She'd already got the waffle-maker out of the cupboard and was now collecting bacon and eggs from the fridge. I honestly don't know why I bother saying anything because no one takes the slightest bit of notice of me around here.

'About five,' I replied.

Chloe and Danni were my best friends at school, and they were coming for pizza and DVDs that evening. I knew there was *one* DVD we *definitely* wouldn't be watching. *Hannah Fleetwood, Future Captain of the England Women's Football Team...*

Actually, thinking about it, Chloe and Danni were the *only* friends I had at school. I hadn't said anything to Mum and Dad, but it had taken me a long, long time to get settled in at Greenwood. For the first six months we'd still been living in our old house, and it was a long journey across town to get to Greenwood, so I hadn't really joined in any after-school activities. Also, Greenwood was *really* big compared to my primary school, and there were so many pupils and teachers. Even now, after eight months in year 7, I swear that there are still times when I get lost among the endless corridors.

I hadn't wanted to go to Greenwood at all. I'd wanted to go to the secondary school all my year 6 friends were going to. Dad had said no, though, because he thought Greenwood was better. Don't ask me how he managed to get me a place at Greenwood, though – it's a very popular school, and we weren't even living in the right area of Melfield at the time. But that's my dad for you. He's a fixer. He always gets what he wants.

'Which of your team-mates are going on the course with you this week, Hannie?' Dad asked, joining me at the table.

'Well, there's Grace Kennedy and Georgie Taylor and—'

'Grace?' Dad frowned.

'She's the slim blonde girl who plays up front, isn't she?' Mum chimed in. 'The one who looks like a model?'

'Yep, that's Grace,' I replied.

'How many goals has she scored this season, then?' Dad asked.

I shrugged. 'About twenty-five, I think.'

'Really.' Dad frowned. 'That's a lot more than you, Hannah. You've only scored eight.'

'Dad!' I rolled my eyes. 'Grace is our star striker. I'm a midfielder. Of *course* she's going to score more goals than me.'

Dad shook his finger at me. 'I'll have you know, young lady, that Cristiano Ronaldo scored over forty goals in all competitions during the 2007–08 season.'

I was silent. I was absolutely sure that Cristiano Ronaldo didn't have *any* of his family standing on the touchline yelling at him during every match.

'Georgie's your goalie, isn't she?' Dad asked. 'The tall girl with the attitude?'

I grinned and nodded. That was a pretty accurate summing-up of Georgie. Although Grace was officially our captain, Georgie often screamed at us from the goalmouth. To be honest, I was actually a little bit scared of her.

'She's not bad,' Dad said grudgingly. 'She's pretty fearless, which is good in a goalie. But being foolhardy is a different matter.'

I knew what he meant. Georgie had given away a penalty only last week when she'd shoulder charged the other team's striker. She'd then argued furiously with the ref and got sent off.

'Then there's Jasmin Sharma, Katy Nowak and Lauren Bell,' I said. 'Lauren and Jasmin play in midfield with me, and Katy's our centre-back.'

'Yes, Katy's a very good player,' Dad said approvingly. 'Quick and clever and solid in defence. She's scored a few goals this season with her head too.'

'Yes.' I felt rather jealous. Katy Nowak *was* a good player, but I wished that Dad would say things like that about *me* more often.

'So you've got five training days this week, Monday to Friday, and then the girls who attended the course are playing a match on Saturday morning,' Dad said. 'Is that right?'

'Mm,' I mumbled, picking up my new earrings and studying them intently. I knew what was coming.

'Are you *sure* parents aren't allowed to attend any of the sessions?' asked Dad. 'Just to watch?'

'I don't think so,' I said, not looking at him. The training sessions *were* closed to spectators, so I wasn't *really* lying. But we'd already been told that parents would be allowed to come to the Saturday-morning game, if they liked. I wouldn't admit that, though, unless Dad asked me directly.

I hated to hear the disappointment in his voice. But,

just for once, I wanted to be left alone to enjoy playing without someone constantly screaming at me.

I was saved by the bell. The doorbell, actually.

'Ah, this must be the postman.' Dad jumped to his feet. 'I'm sure he's staggering under the weight of lots of birthday cards for the future captain of the England women's team!'

He dashed off down the hall towards the front door.

'It's a shame we can't come and see you play,' Mum said casually, breaking eggs into the sizzling oil.

'Yes.' I wondered if Mum was suspicious, but she didn't say anything more.

The kitchen door opened and my half-sister, Olivia, walked in, followed by Dad.

'It wasn't the postman,' Dad said, rather obviously. 'It was Olivia.'

'Hi,' Olivia said languidly, flapping her fingers in a half-hearted wave at me and Mum. She glanced at the cards and presents on the table and did a rather elaborate double-take. 'Oh God, Hannah, is it your birthday? Sorry, I'd forgotten.'

'Yeah, right,' I said under my breath.

There was *no way* Olivia didn't know it was my birthday because her mum, Carol, Dad's first wife, had popped round yesterday with a present for me. But Olivia simply can't bear anyone else to be the centre of attention, except her.

Olivia and I have never got on. We don't even look alike – honestly, you'd never *believe* we have the same dad. Olivia's quite petite with black hair and very dark eyes, and I'm taller and have brown hair and green eyes. She's three years older than me, and I know she thinks I'm seriously strange just because I love playing football. Well, that's fine with me because I think she's an airhead who adores making a complete drama out of anything and everything. I like make-up and clothes and shopping and stuff just as much as Olivia does, but when she's around, somehow I just seem to start behaving more like a tomboy. Probably because I know it winds Olivia up, ha ha. She used to come and stay with us regularly when she was younger, but now that we've moved and live much closer to her and her mum, Olivia just pops in whenever she feels like it.

'So Mum and I had, like, *another* row this morning.' Olivia draped herself over one of the kitchen chairs and rested her black knee-length boots on the edge of the round table. I saw Mum wince, but she didn't say anything. Neither did Dad.

That's *another* thing that annoys me. Dad hardly ever criticises Olivia. But he's always going on at me, not just about football but about *everything*.

Dad sighed. 'What is it this time, sweetie?'

'Oh, she treats me like a child, Dad!' Olivia said impatiently. 'I'm, like, *no*, Mum, I've done my homework and you don't need to check my books, thank you very much. But she won't *leave* it. She's just not chilled like you, Dad.'

'Dad's really strict about me doing *my* homework on time,' I muttered.

Olivia ignored me.

'It's getting worse, Dad,' she said plaintively. 'We're arguing all the time now. So this morning I just said, well, I've had enough of this, yeah?'

She smiled up at Dad, fluttering her eyelashes (they were fake, I noted).

'And so I told Mum I wanted to come and live here, with you.'

CHAPTER TWO

'You've got to be joking!' I burst out, and then blushed as Dad gave me one of his looks. Olivia also glared at me.

'Oh, thanks *so* much for that very helpful comment, Hannah,' she remarked in an icy tone. 'I was talking to *my* dad, not to you.'

I had to bite my lip to stop myself from saying anything more. I was reminded of a bitter argument Olivia and I had when I was seven years old and Olivia was ten. The argument was about which one of us was Dad's favourite daughter, and I think Olivia started it, although I can't really remember.

Mum was furious when we wouldn't stop yelling at each other, and sent us up to our rooms, but Olivia, as usual, was determined to have the last word. She had sneaked out and slipped a note under my bedroom door.

Dad loves me more than he loves you, Olivia had written. *He told me so.*

I had never forgotten it.

I glanced at Mum, hoping she'd back me up, but she was standing there with her mouth open and an egg in either hand. If that had been me, I think I would've thrown them at Olivia.

'Livvy, sweetheart, *please*,' Dad said. 'You can't march in here and drop a bombshell like that. What about your mother? She'd be really hurt if you moved out—'

'Oh, Dad, get real!' Olivia broke in impatiently. 'Mum won't care, not now she's seeing Martin.' She jumped up and put her arms around Dad and I wrinkled my nose in disgust. Olivia was a grand master of emotional blackmail. 'I miss you, Dad,' she wheedled. 'Mum would be cool with me coming to live with you, I know she would.'

Dad hesitated, and I felt my tummy tying itself into knots. There was just no way I could live with my über-spoilt half-sister. I would have to run away or hire a hitman.

'Olivia, you know I need to speak to your mother before we even think about making any big decisions like this,' Dad mumbled, looking very uncomfortable. 'Now, I'm taking Hannah to her football course after breakfast, so I'll drop you off at home on the way—'

Olivia's face darkened. 'Oh, well, if *football's* more important than my future and the rest of my whole life,' she declaimed dramatically, 'then I guess I'll just have to be a good little girl and put up with it without complaining, like I always do.'

I almost laughed but just about managed not to, as Olivia swept across the kitchen, nose in the air.

'Livvy, *please*—' Dad began.

'Oh, like, *whatever*,' Olivia snapped, and we heard her stomp off down the hallway towards the front door.

'I'll get her out of the garage and talk to the car,' Dad said distractedly, rushing after her. 'I mean, I'll get the car out of the garage and talk to her. You enjoy your birthday breakfast, Hannah.'

I only half-finished Mum's man-sized meal (actually, it would have fed three men for a week), but I deliberately didn't hurry to collect my jacket and my sports bag. *Why should Olivia have it all her own way?* I thought sulkily. She was a major pain in the butt. I was only a few years younger than her, and *I* didn't behave that way. I didn't dare. So why should Olivia get away with it?

'Mum,' I said anxiously, '*you* don't want Olivia to move in, do you?'

'Well, it *would* be a bit disruptive, I admit,' Mum replied. Then she turned a little pink as if she felt she'd said too much. 'But you heard your dad, Hannie. Nothing can be decided quickly, so we'll just have to wait and see for the moment.'

I didn't bother to say anything more. Mum might object at first, but eventually she'd go along with whatever Dad wanted, so there was no point.

Miserably I trudged down the hallway, imagining what it would be like to have Olivia here all the time. The two of us at each other's throats, and Mum and Dad trying to keep the peace. It would be like living in a sitcom, except it wouldn't be the least bit funny.

Dad and Olivia were sitting in the car talking when I climbed into the back seat. Olivia looked a lot happier, which made me feel even more depressed. What had Dad been promising her?

'Honestly, Dad, I can walk home,' Olivia said as we pulled off the drive. Note she only offered *after* Dad had started up the car and backed it out onto the road. 'I don't want Hannah to be late for her football course because of me.'

Ooh, that is so Olivia! She always comes over all sugary-sweet after she's been a total pain.

'Oh, it's only a couple of minutes out of the way,' Dad replied. 'We won't be very late.'

'Are you OK with that, Hannah?' Olivia enquired, turning to glance at me.

Nooo! I am SO not OK with that. Go away! I hate you!!

'Yes,' I said.

Olivia smiled – well, it was more of a smirk if you want to be accurate. Then she ignored me completely and talked to Dad until we reached her mum's house.

I didn't care. I sat silently in the back of the car, hugging my sports bag. Olivia always thought that she was better than me because she was Dad's favourite and oh-so-clever, but she didn't know *everything*. In fact, not even Mum and Dad knew everything about me either...

I unzipped my bag slightly and peeked inside. The pink envelope, my special, secret birthday card, the one no one else knew about, was still there. I'd open it later when I was alone.

'Dad, you won't forget about the shopping trip you promised me?' Olivia said when we stopped outside her home.

I rolled my eyes. I knew there had to be a bribe in there *somewhere*!

'I won't forget,' Dad promised.

'And the other thing,' Olivia persisted. 'Moving in with you. Will you talk to Mum?'

'Yes, but it's going to take time, sweetie—'

'Oh, Dad, for God's sake!' Olivia snapped. 'I can't stay with Mum. She's driving me mad!' She flung open the car door, and Dad winced as it narrowly missed a nearby tree. 'If you won't do something about it, then I will!'

'Olivia, what do you mean?' Dad began. But Olivia had made her grand exit from the car, leaving the door wide open. She kicked open the garden gate and stalked up the path. It was impressive, except that she tripped on an uneven paving slab and almost went head over heels. *Tee hee.*

'Right,' Dad said in a very fake cheerful voice when

Olivia had slammed the front door pointedly behind her. 'Let's get you to your football course, Hannie.'

We drove off in silence towards Melfield United's ground near the centre of town. I longed to know what Dad was going to do about Olivia, but there was no point in asking because he wouldn't tell me.

'Look, Hannah,' Dad suddenly remarked, when we were just a mile or so away from the ground, 'isn't that your goalie over there?'

I glanced out of the window and saw Georgie Taylor racing down the street. You couldn't miss her – she was tall and skinny and she had all this fantastic black hair flying out behind her. As I watched, Georgie swerved neatly around a mum with a pushchair, hurdled over a discarded McDonald's bag and dodged around the corner.

'She's late,' Dad said. 'We'll pick her up.'

Dad swung around the corner and we stopped a few metres ahead of Georgie. I buzzed the window down and stuck out my head.

'Hi, Georgie, do you want a lift?' I called as she drew alongside.

Grinning widely, Georgie immediately scooted over to us.

'Ta very much,' she said, jumping into the back seat

next to me. 'I couldn't find my boots this morning because Luke, one of my brothers, had hidden them – ha ha, great joke, *not* childish and immature at all, oh no – and then the stupid bus broke down and I wanted to kick someone or something very hard.'

'Stick to a football,' I suggested. 'That way you won't get done for GBH.'

Georgie giggled, wrinkling her nose.

'This is a bit of a flash car, isn't it?' she said, glancing around Dad's new silver BMW. I felt a bit embarrassed, but I was starting to get used to Georgie by now. I've realised that she always says exactly what she thinks.

'Thank you,' Dad replied, turning briefly to smile at her, 'I think.'

I wonder if Dad would prefer me to be more like Georgie – you know, fearless and upfront and never afraid to say what she thinks? The thought upset me, so I pushed it aside.

'Are you looking forward to the training course this week, Georgie?' Dad said, as we reached the ground and drove into the car park. 'It's a shame we aren't allowed to come and watch, isn't it? How do your parents feel about that?'

Horrified, I froze in my seat. I stared at

Georgie, dumb appeal in my eyes.

'Well, actually—' Georgie began chattily.

Then she glanced at me and broke off. I saw a frown flit across her face.

'Oh!' Georgie suddenly groaned, scrabbling for the door handle. 'Sorry, Mr Fleetwood, I feel sick!'

'What?' Dad swung round in his seat, looking worried for his new leather upholstery. 'But we've stopped moving!'

'Doesn't matter,' Georgie moaned as she threw the door open. 'It's that new-car smell. It's making me ill!' And she stumbled out into the gravelled car park, clutching her stomach.

'See you later, Dad,' I mumbled with relief, trying not to laugh. I grabbed Georgie's bag and my own, and dashed after her.

As Dad drove away, Georgie straightened up and winked at me.

'And the Oscar for Best Actress in a pretending-to-spew scene goes to...'

'Thanks,' I said.

Georgie shrugged. 'Forget it,' she said breezily, kicking at the gravel with the toe of her battered Nike trainers. 'He's pretty full-on, isn't he? Your dad, I mean.'

I sighed. 'Yep. Pretty full-on.'

'I couldn't be doing with all that yelling and screaming at every game,' Georgie remarked as we went to check in at reception. 'Doesn't it bother you?'

I stared at her in amazement. 'Well, duh, of *course* it does.'

'Why don't you do something about it, then?' Georgie challenged me, her dark eyes searching and direct.

I could feel myself coming over all hot and red-faced and embarrassed, and I couldn't look at her. It was a simple, straightforward question, but I couldn't answer it without getting into all sorts of complicated family stuff.

'My oldest brother, Adey, is on the books here as an apprentice,' Georgie remarked as the receptionist searched for our names on the course list.

'Really?' I was impressed. 'You're a bit of a football-crazy family, then, aren't you?'

Georgie nodded. She looked as if she was going to say something more, but then thought better of it.

I'd been to Melfield United's ground lots of times. Although Dad and I were Arsenal through and through, we also liked to support our local team, who were in League Two. I'd never been behind the scenes before, and I was looking forward to having a quick nose around. But the receptionist told us that we were late and to hurry, so Georgie and I dashed along the corridor towards the changing-rooms, following the signs which read, *Football Course for Girls – this way.* I was actually glad, though, because it meant Georgie didn't have the opportunity to ask me any more awkward questions.

The changing-room was painted in blue and white, Melfield United's colours. It was packed with girls, and the noise was deafening. I recognised some players from rival teams – I spotted Sally Burton, the Seventrees captain, and the Franklin twins and a couple of others from Deepdale Under-Thirteens, as well as a few more familiar faces.

'Listen for the loudest noise, and that's where our lot will be,' Georgie said drily as we stood in the doorway.

Right on cue we heard shrieks of laughter. I glanced across the changing-room and saw Grace, Lauren, Jasmin and Katy gathered in a huddle beside the lockers. They had already changed into their purple strips and now they were staring down at a mobile phone that Lauren was holding. At that moment, though, Grace (or the Perfect Princess, as

I secretly call her) glanced up and spotted us.

'Georgie! Hannah!' she called, waving wildly, her long blonde hair swinging. 'Over here!'

Although I'd been playing for the team for a few weeks now, I still felt a bit shy as Georgie and I went to join them. It wasn't because the other girls weren't welcoming or because I was an outsider. In fact, I got the impression that these five girls, at least, didn't see much of each other away from the team. Georgie and Grace were in the same class at Greenwood High, so I think they knew each other quite well, and I'd heard that Jasmin and Lauren had been to the same primary school. Like me, Katy hadn't been playing for the team for very long either, and although she too was quiet, I don't think it was because she was shy. Even if they weren't close mates, all the girls seemed relaxed and confident around one another. I was the only one who wasn't. But I've never been that great at getting to know people and making friends. God, how sad am I?

'You two have to see this!' Jasmin exclaimed, clutching my arm. Her dark brown eyes were round with delight. 'Lauren has downloaded this YouTube video of someone teaching their guinea pig to do tricks. It's amazing!'

Lauren winked at us, flicking back her glossy blonde curls. 'This guinea pig is *the* cleverest guinea pig in the whole world,' she announced solemnly. 'It is possibly the most intelligent pet in existence today.'

'Really?' Georgie said, not sounding impressed at all. She had already unzipped her black and white hoodie, and underneath she wore her Spurs shirt. Well, nobody's perfect.

'Oh, *yes*,' Jasmin replied earnestly. 'This guinea pig can turn somersaults, walk a tightrope and play the piano. And its owner is actually teaching it how to make a cup of tea, can you believe it?'

I stared at her in amazement. 'Is that true?' I asked. I had already summed Jasmin up as very sweet, but rather ditsy. She was the same on the football field. Although she was a skilful player, she got distracted easily and could be a bit clumsy.

'Absolutely,' Jasmin assured me in a solemn voice as she scraped her wavy black hair into a high ponytail. 'It switches the kettle on and it gets the teabag in its little teeth and—'

'That doesn't sound very hygienic,' I pointed out, noticing that Lauren's baby-blue eyes were dancing and her lips twitching. 'So how does it pour the water into the cup?'

Jasmin looked blank and I grinned. Meanwhile, Lauren, Grace and Katy collapsed into uproarious giggles.

'Jasmin, you are *such* a dipstick!' Grace gasped. 'It's not *real*. Someone's been messing around with special effects, that's all.'

Jasmin looked incredibly disappointed. Then she laughed too.

'Lauren, I think I *will* have to kill you,' she said. She made a grab for Lauren, who squeaked and ducked behind Grace, still giggling. 'The only question is how? Death by slow torture or a quick and painless exit?'

'Get the guinea pig to do it,' I suggested, and this time everyone almost split their sides laughing, even Jasmin. It gave me a warm feeling inside to be able to make them crease up like that.

'Let's have a little less noise around here and a little more action,' said a dour voice from the doorway.

We all glanced round and I realised that the changing-room was almost empty by now. We'd been having such a laugh, I hadn't seen that most of the other girls had gone out on to the pitch. A stocky woman in a grey tracksuit was standing just inside the door and fixing us with what could only be described as a sour look.

'I'm Martha, one of your coaches,' the woman went on glumly, sounding as if she wished she was a thousand miles away. 'You should be changed and ready by now. Get on with it, please.'

I was the only one who wasn't changed – even Georgie was in her strip by now. I blushed and began to fumble my way out of my clothes.

'Sorry, coach,' Grace said politely, flashing her model-girl smile. 'We'll be right out.'

But Martha wasn't buying into the Perfect Princess effect. She simply nodded and walked off.

'And hello and welcome to you too,' Lauren said, poking her tongue out at Martha's back. 'Don't say we've got to put up with Martha the Misery for a whole week?'

'Come on, guys, there's no point in getting up the coach's nose on the first day,' Grace said sensibly, slipping her silver bangles off her wrists. She's the oldest and the most grown up of all of us on the team. But then she's beautiful and she's clever and she's our best player and yet she's a nice person too. When I'd turned up for my first Springhill Stars training session, feeling all nervous, Grace had immediately come over to say hello. Maybe *I'd* be more grown up, if I had everything that Grace had going for her.

Jasmin turned to me. 'Shall we wait for you, Hannah?'

'Nah, you go ahead,' I muttered, as I struggled out of my tracksuit. 'I'll catch you up.'

'Bet you'd rather have Martha the Misery yelling at you than your dad, though, wouldn't you, Hannah?' Lauren said with a knowing grin.

'I said, let's go,' Grace repeated, eyeballing Lauren sternly. She gave the younger girl a gentle shove and Lauren skipped cheerfully over to the door. Although she was small and petite, Lauren was just as loud, bouncy and cheeky on the football field as she was off it, but she could also lose her temper at the drop of a hat, and she got sent off almost as often as Georgie.

I kept my head down as the others followed Lauren and Grace out. I knew that they probably all thought the same as Georgie, and that they couldn't understand why I put up with Dad's behaviour at our matches. I squirmed inwardly as I realised they must feel sorry for me. Maybe they even laughed at me, just a little. It was *so* embarrassing.

'Are you OK, Hannah?'

I looked up into Katy Nowak's steady brown eyes. I hadn't even noticed that she'd stayed behind when the others had left.

'I'm fine,' I said, digging my boots out of my bag. 'You go. No point us all getting into trouble.'

Katy shrugged. 'I'll wait for you,' she said easily. 'I have to tie my hair back anyway.' She took an elasticated band and a comb from the plastic bag she always brought her kit in. Then she went over to the mirror, humming quietly to herself, and began to brush her dark brown hair.

I didn't know much about Katy at all, just that she was Polish and that her family had only been in this country for a couple of years. But there was something comforting and solid about her that made me think she would be a good and loyal friend. I liked her.

As I sat down to lace up my boots, I caught a glimpse of the pink envelope at the bottom of my bag. I had my secret, and it was all mine, something just for *me*. But I also knew that this situation couldn't go on for ever. Sometime, soon, I was going to have to confess what I'd been up to for the last couple of weeks. The thought of telling Dad what

I'd been doing made me feel sick. He'd never understand. He'd go *ballistic*.

And now, as if things weren't bad enough, Olivia was making my life a million times worse. I knew exactly what my darling half-sister was like, and I had absolutely no doubt that eventually she'd get her own way and sweet-talk Dad into letting her move in.

So, it looked like I had two BIG problems on my hands, and absolutely no idea what to do about either of them...

CHAPTER THREE

Katy and I clattered down the corridor towards the players' tunnel, the only sound the noise of our studs on the floor. I think this was the first time I'd ever been alone with her, and you know what, I'd gone all shy again and couldn't think of a single thing to say. I am *so* rubbish at small talk!

'Er – are you looking forward to this footie course, then, Katy?' I asked hesitantly.

Katy nodded. 'Very much,' she replied. Her English was really good – much better than my Polish, believe me! She had an accent, but it sounded quite cute. 'I thought I might not be allowed to come.'

'Oh?' I said. 'Why not?' Then I could have kicked myself for being so nosey. It was pretty obvious that Katy was a very private person. *Why* do I always seem to say the wrong thing with people I don't know so well?

Katy shrugged. 'Oh, family stuff,' was all she said. But from the tone of her voice, it was almost like I'd hit a barrier with a big sign saying, KEEP OUT – PRIVATE AND PERSONAL.

We came out on to the pitch, where twenty-two other girls were milling around, chatting and punting footballs to each other. Because Melfield United wasn't a big club, the stadium wasn't very large, but it was a lot bigger than the local college field, where we usually played our home matches. The rows of seats were in the team's colours, blue and white.

Martha was standing on the touchline with a man who, like her, was also wearing a grey tracksuit. She glanced pointedly at her watch as Katy and I hurried over to join the others.

Grace and Jasmin were leaning against one of the goalposts, chatting. Grace was admiring the glittery purple nail varnish Jasmin was wearing. Meanwhile, Lauren was standing in goal and Georgie was placing a ball on the penalty-spot.

'Why are *you* practising penalties, Georgie?' Katy asked, looking amused. 'You're a goalkeeper.'

'I want to be a good all-rounder, not just a one-trick pony,' Georgie retorted. 'I *might* just have to take a penalty one day.' She rolled her eyes at Lauren. 'Come on, Lauren, make yourself bigger.'

'I'm doing my best!' Lauren said crossly, doing star jumps on the goal-line and waving her arms around. She looked even more petite, standing between the huge goalposts.

Georgie blasted the ball at the goal and it flew high over the bar.

'Perhaps you meant make the *goal* bigger?' Lauren suggested with a smirk as Georgie scowled.

The deafening blast of a whistle made us all spin round.

'Right, we've wasted quite enough time,' Martha called briskly. 'Let's make a start.'

We all gathered around Martha and the other coach, who introduced himself as Mike Andrews.

'Girls, we'd like to welcome you to the first day of our intensive training course,' Mike said, smiling warmly at us. 'You've all been chosen to attend this week because your team coaches think you're good players who will benefit from a bit of extra coaching. So just keep that in mind when Martha and I are running your legs off! We're going to be doing some drills that you'll be familiar with from your regular training sessions, but there'll be a lot of exciting new stuff too...'

I tried to concentrate on what Mike was saying, but annoyingly my mind kept drifting. I just couldn't help it. OK, I knew that sometime soon my secret would come out, one way or another, and then I'd have to deal with all the hassle, however awful it was. But Olivia coming to live with us was a whole other thing, and just as scary in its own way. She could be there for *years*. I'd get up every morning, and she'd be there. I'd come home from school, and she'd be there. I'd—

'Hannah!' Grace was whispering urgently in my ear, 'Get into line – we're warming up!'

With a start, I realised that everyone else was lining up in twos at the side of the pitch. Under Martha's beady eye, Grace ushered me quickly over to the end of the queue of players.

'You can be my partner, Hannah,' Grace murmured as Martha continued to stare hard at me. 'Are you OK?'

'Fine,' I said automatically, as Mike began to lead

us on a controlled jog around the pitch. I realised that Grace was trying to look after me, and I was grateful. That was typical Grace. She was just so *nice*. 'Er – I didn't quite catch what we're supposed to be doing—'

'Just watch me and do what I do,' Grace replied in a low voice. 'And, Hannah – Martha's already got her eye on you, so just be careful, all right?'

I nodded as Martha joined the end of the line right behind us. I'd been looking forward to this football course for ages, and it was *so* like my evil half-sister to do something to ruin it, and on my birthday too. Especially when I was already worrying about having to confess my secret to Mum and Dad—

'Header!' Martha yelled behind us, almost making me jump out of my skin.

Grace and everyone else jumped up and made a heading movement and I just about managed to do the same without being too far behind them. Then we continued to jog around the pitch.

Anyway, there was nothing I could do, I thought gloomily. I just had to hope that Olivia changed her mind and decided to stay with her mum—

'High knees!' Martha roared, breathing down my

neck. Again, I was a fraction behind everyone else and I could hear Martha tutting loudly behind me. 'Come on, Hannah, get those legs up!'

By the time we'd warmed up and stretched and done a few fun drills, though, I started to get into the training session. Mike and Martha wanted to start with basic controlling, turning and passing so that they could check our technique, but I didn't actually care *what* we were doing. Playing football or even just having a ball at my feet and messing around with it, had always cleared my head, whatever else was on my mind. That was something I'd forgotten, though, ever since Dad had taken on his self-appointed role as my motivational coach. It was great to get that feeling back and to realise that it was still there, especially after what had happened earlier with Olivia.

I even managed to impress Martha. She and Mike had marked out zones with plastic cones, and one of us inside each zone was given a blue bib to wear. The person wearing the bib then had to try and get the ball away from the other players while they passed it around the zones. When it was my turn to wear the bib, I was determined to do well, and I did.

'Ah, I see you've finally woken up, Hannah,'

Martha remarked grudgingly as I tackled Rachel Franklin and swept the ball neatly away from her. 'I was wondering why your coach had recommended you for this course. There's hope for you yet.'

'Thanks, Martha,' I said.

'Don't get carried away, though,' Martha replied sternly. 'You've still got a lot to learn and a long way to go yet.'

'She's a charmer, isn't she?' Lauren whispered as we walked off the pitch together at the end of the session. My muscles were aching gently, but it wasn't an unpleasant feeling. 'If you gave her a doughnut, she'd moan about the hole in the middle.'

'Mike's nice, though,' Grace remarked. She was behind us with Georgie, Jasmin and Katy.

'Yeah, I think the two of them have got a kind of good-cop, bad-cop thing going on,' Georgie added.

'Look, it's only just after twelve.' Jasmin pointed up at the clock above the players' tunnel as we passed underneath. 'We finished early, didn't we? My mum's not picking me up till around twelve-thirty.'

'Let's go to the café,' Lauren suggested. 'Milkshakes all round?'

'Great,' I agreed eagerly. The morning had been huge fun, and it had taken my mind right off my problems. I'd enjoyed being with the other girls too, and I didn't want it to end.

'I think I'd better go straight home,' Katy said quietly from the back.

Lauren spun round to glance at her. 'Why?' she asked bluntly.

Katy looked slightly taken aback. 'Well, I have things to do—'

'Oh, stay, just for ten minutes!' Lauren wheedled, linking her arm through Katy's. Despite my anxiety, I had to smile. Lauren was just like an eager, bouncy little puppy – you couldn't help liking her. 'You can't go yet. I've been practising my Martha the Misery impression, and I want you *all* to see it.'

Lauren stopped, put her hands on her hips, hunched her shoulders and pursed her mouth so that it looked like she was sucking a lemon.

'Now that's not bad, Hannah, but don't get above yourself,' Lauren announced in an almost exact imitation of Martha's morose tone. 'You've got a long way to go before you're as good as Mia Hamm.'

We were all in fits before she'd even finished.

'Move along there, girls.' We almost jumped out of our skins when we heard the real Martha's voice close behind us. But that only made us giggle all the more, I'm afraid.

'Do you think she overheard me?' Lauren whispered as we scurried off to the changing-rooms, still laughing. 'I am so dead if she did.'

'Yes, you'll probably get ten thousand press-ups tomorrow as a punishment,' Jasmin replied. 'Do you think Martha will crack a smile or not before the end of the week, is the question.'

'I think we should set a challenge,' Grace suggested as we pushed our way through the crowded changing-room. 'Let's see who can make Martha smile first.'

'That'll be Jasmin,' Georgie predicted confidently. 'We just need to wait for her to trip up over her own feet, like she's always doing. Martha'll never keep a straight face then.'

'Are you saying I'm *clumsy*, Georgie Taylor?' Jasmin squeaked indignantly. She spun round to glare at Georgie and accidentally stuck her foot inside an open sports bag left lying on the floor.

'Oops! Sorry!' Jasmin gasped at the bag's owner. She tried to lift her foot out, and only succeeded in getting her boot caught in one of the handle loops. Giggling helplessly, Grace and Katy pulled her free.

'What a shame Martha wasn't here,' Georgie said, 'You'd have won the challenge already, Jasmin.'

We all got changed. I wiggled out of my strip and boots, threw on my tracksuit and trainers, undid my ponytail and brushed out my hair. I don't bother with clothes or make-up much when I'm at footie training. But Lauren, Jasmin and Grace were doing the whole deal with jewellery, sparkly hair-slides and heels. Meanwhile, Georgie was sighing and glancing pointedly at her watch.

'Do you have a problem, Georgie?' Lauren enquired with a cheeky grin, slipping her purple T-shirt over her head. 'Some of us like to make an effort, you know.'

Grinning, Georgie poked her tongue out at her. 'I'm not into all that pink, glittery, girly stuff,' she retorted.

'No, you're quite plain and ordinary, aren't you, Georgie?' Jasmin agreed, tucking her hair inside a crocheted white beanie hat. Then she looked horrified as we started giggling. 'I didn't mean *that*!' Jasmin spluttered. 'I just meant that Georgie likes plain and ordinary clothes, not that she's *actually* plain and ordinary.'

'Thanks, Jasmin,' Georgie said drily, raising an eyebrow. 'With friends like you, who needs enemies!'

Jasmin started giggling herself now, and we left the changing-room, still laughing.

'You've cheered up a whole lot, Hannah,' Grace remarked. 'You looked miles away when the training session started.'

I nodded. 'Yeah, I was,' I admitted. 'It was just—' I had to stop myself from saying too much. I had no intention of telling the other girls *everything* that was going on in my life. I mean, they were nice enough, but I still hardly knew them. No way was I sharing my *special* secret. 'My half-sister, Olivia, is being a pain at the moment, that's all. She wants to move in with us.'

'Ooh, Ugly Sister alert!' Jasmin said sympathetically. 'I suppose that makes you Cinderella, huh, Hannah?'

'I guess,' I said, forcing a smile. 'Except I don't have a fairy godmother.'

'So why don't you like Olivia, then, Hannah?' Lauren asked, as we headed towards the café, which was at the front of the ground near the car park.

'Well, she doesn't like me either!' I said, trying to laugh it off. 'And once—'

I had to stop myself abruptly again. I had just been about to tell the story of Olivia's note under my bedroom door all those years ago. But I definitely didn't want to go into my family history. That could be dangerous. Lauren was staring at me with open curiosity but I looked away, not meeting her eyes. 'Oh, never mind,' I mumbled uncomfortably.

The café was a retro 50s diner with red leather booths and pictures of Marilyn Monroe and impossibly big American cars on the walls.

'Look, corner booth for six next to the window,' Georgie pointed out as we piled inside. 'Get it, quick, before the Deepdale crew beat us to it!'

We charged across the café and snaffled the booth from under the noses of the Deepdale players. Jasmin managed to bump into another table and send the salt cellar flying, but there was no damage done.

'Georgie and I will get the drinks in,' Grace said, taking charge as usual, 'and you can all settle up with us afterwards.'

'Banana,' Lauren said.

'Strawberry,' I added.

'Banana or strawberry or chocolate?' Jasmin mused. 'I'll have banana. No, I'll have strawberry. No, chocolate, definitely.'

Katy shook her head. 'Nothing for me,' she said.

'Don't you have any money?' Lauren asked.

'No,' Katy replied quietly.

'I'll lend you some.' Lauren dived into her bag and began scrabbling around.

'No, thank you.' Katy flushed a little. Although she spoke quietly, there was a steely look in her eyes which said, *don't mess with me.* 'I don't want anything. Really.'

Lauren shrugged, looking a bit put out. 'Please yourself.'

Georgie and Grace went off, with Jasmin calling after them, 'I don't want chocolate after all, I'll have banana.'

'By the way, Jasmin, how did your cousin's wedding go last Sunday?' Lauren asked, tucking her blonde hair behind her ears.

'Oh, it was *really* fun!' Jasmin replied enthusiastically. 'Look, I have photos.' She took out her phone and flicked through to the pictures menu. 'Do you like my outfit?'

'It's gorgeous,' I said, studying the photo. Jasmin was wearing a beautiful, floaty, long skirt with a matching top. The suit was peacock-blue, embroidered with silver, and she had a silver chiffon-type scarf around her neck. 'I *love* Indian clothes. They're so pretty.'

'You'll have to come round to mine for a fashion session sometime, then,' Jasmin invited me cheerfully. 'I have *loads*.'

'Cool,' I agreed happily.

Just then Georgie and Grace came back with the tray. There were six paper cups on it.

'I bought a large one and asked them to split it between two small cups,' Georgie said, pushing one of them across the table to Katy. 'Don't make me beg or I'll be crushed.'

Katy hesitated. For a moment I thought she was going to refuse, but then she smiled and took the paper cup a little reluctantly.

'So, what's everyone doing these holidays, apart from the footie course?' Grace asked, as she and Georgie squeezed into the booth.

'Mum and I are going to Florida next week,' Lauren said, slurping noisily on her straw. 'But I've got enough holiday homework for six people.'

'Which school do you go to?' I asked.

Lauren pulled a face. 'Riverton Hill.'

I managed to stop my mouth falling open. Riverton Hill was seriously posh. Dad had thought about sending me there instead of Greenwood, but had decided we couldn't really afford the fees for the next seven years.

'That's the school with the fashion statement uniform, isn't it?' Georgie remarked. 'Green blazer, blue skirt, stripy tie and a beret, anyone?'

'Don't!' Lauren groaned, kicking out at Georgie under the table.

'I didn't even feel that, by the way,' Georgie said with her trademark wide grin.

'That's because she kicked *me* instead,' Jasmin yelped, massaging her ankle. 'I haven't got much holiday homework, but I know my parents want me to study every day. I practically had to get down on my knees and *plead* with them to let me come on this course.'

'Do you go to Riverton too?' I asked.

Jasmin shook her head. 'No, Bramfield Girls. I want to play loads of football but I want to do lots of other things too, like go shopping and have sleepovers and see my mates.'

'Back in a minute, guys,' Lauren said, standing up and squeezing past Grace.

'Well, I say stuff homework,' Georgie announced, stirring her milkshake with a straw as Lauren disappeared into the ladies'. 'I'm going to play footie and watch DVDs, and eat my own weight in

Easter eggs. Oh, and annoy my idiot brothers as much as possible. But I do that all year round, anyway.'

'How many brothers have you got?' I asked.

This time it was Georgie's turn to pull a face. 'Three,' she muttered. 'And that's three too many.'

'Do you have any brothers or sisters, Grace?' Katy said. Because she was new to the team, like me, neither of us knew that much about the other girls' home lives. I was curious too.

'I've got a twin sister called Gemma,' Grace replied.

'You're a twin!' I exclaimed, sitting up in my seat. 'Wow! Are you identical? Is she tall and blonde like you?'

Grace nodded.

'Gemma's never come to one of our matches, has she?' Georgie remarked, as Lauren headed back towards us. 'That would be *seriously* weird, seeing the same person on the pitch and in the crowd!'

'Gem doesn't like football,' Grace said.

'It must be so cool to have an identical twin,' Jasmin remarked enviously.

'Yes.' A shadow flitted very briefly across Grace's pretty face, and I wondered why. But before we could ask anything else, her phone started buzzing.

'Oh, sorry,' she apologised quickly, looking anything but sorry as she snatched her phone from the table. In fact, she seemed relieved to have an opportunity to change the subject.

'Someone else's phone is going off,' Georgie pointed out, as just seconds later, we heard a series of loud beeps.

We all dived into our pockets and bags, apart from Grace, who was frowning as she read her message. As I opened my sports bag, I realised it was *my* phone blaring out. Because it was new, I hadn't set my own ringtone or message alert yet, so I didn't recognise it.

'It's me,' I mumbled, feeling a bit embarrassed. 'Sorry.'

Georgie rolled her eyes good-naturedly at me.

'So, about tomorrow, girls,' Jasmin began, her eyes twinkling impishly, 'any ideas how we can cheer Martha up?'

Meanwhile, I was fumbling with my phone, trying to work out the buttons.

New message.

I clicked the *view* button and the message popped up before my disbelieving eyes.

You have a secret!

CHAPTER FOUR

I totally panicked. Instinctively I glanced sideways to make sure that Katy, who was sitting next to me, hadn't read it. Then hiding the phone under the table, away from prying eyes, I quickly pressed *delete*.

The text vanished instantly. Then, in the next second, I realised that I had just lost any chance of finding out who had sent it. I felt sick to the very bottom of my stomach as, with shaking fingers, I thrust the phone into my sports bag again.

The other girls were still laughing and joking about Martha as I sat there, my mind in a total spin. *Think, Hannah! Who could it be? Who could possibly know that I have a secret?*

The answer came to me effortlessly.

Olivia!

It *had* to be Olivia. There was no one else. I had kept my old number for my new phone, and she could easily have got it from Dad.

My mind was whirling with questions I had no answers to. My stomach was churning with dread as I wondered what was going to happen next. *Keep calm, Hannah, and think this through.*

I took a deep breath. It looked like my two big problems had now become one huge, scary nightmare.

How on *earth* had Olivia realised that something was going on? Frantically, I racked my brains. I could only guess that she'd seen or heard something that had aroused her suspicions. We were living close to her and her mum now, so maybe Olivia had caught sight of me in the wrong area of town or something. She could have asked Mum or Dad where I was *supposed* to be at that time, and then put two and two together, maybe?

But the text had said, *You have a secret.* It didn't say, *I know your secret.* That had to mean that Olivia didn't know any of the details, didn't it? So why send the text at all?

The answer popped into my head immediately. Because Olivia couldn't resist boasting that she was on my trail. And because she wanted me to worry. She was going to make me sweat for a while. She'd enjoy that. Knowing Olivia, she'd also assume that she was clever enough to find out what was going on, even though she'd given me a warning and put me on my guard...

'Don't even *try* to make me smile, you horrible lot – I only ever smile on my birthday and at Christmas!'

Lauren was doing her impersonation of Martha again, and the other girls were falling about, laughing. No one had noticed yet that I wasn't joining in.

Perhaps Olivia was playing for time, not just because she wanted me to worry, but also because she wanted to find out *exactly* what my secret was. Then maybe she would use it to blackmail me. Get me to tell Dad that I *really* wanted her to move in with us, otherwise she'd spill the beans and drop me right in it. Oh, that would be just like her...

On the other hand, if Olivia *did* find out the details, maybe then she'd just go straight for the jugular and tell Dad everything, immediately. Either way, I was in big trouble...

But even if I managed to outwit Olivia, she was bound to alert Dad that *something* was going on, when she'd finished amusing herself by messing with my head. And if Dad asked me straight out for an explanation, wanting to know if I'd been deceiving him and Mum in any way, I'd cave in immediately and confess. I was certain I would.

So it was a win-win situation for Olivia. Whatever happened – whether Olivia discovered everything and told Dad, whether I confessed to Dad myself or whether Olivia announced that she knew I had some sort of secret, but not the details – I'd be in trouble and she'd be Little Miss Favourite Daughter. It was sickening.

'Hannah? What's the matter? Are you all right?'

I could hear a voice coming from what seemed a very long way away. I forced myself to focus and glanced up at Grace. She was staring at me, a concerned look on her face.

'I'm fine,' I mumbled, wishing I was on my own so that I could get my head straight and calm down a bit.

'We've never done this before, have we?' Lauren

remarked. She took her straw out of her cup and blew a blob of milkshake at Jasmin.

'Lauren!' Jasmin squealed crossly, wiping a splash of milkshake off her nose.

'I think every five-year-old's done *that* before,' Grace said.

'I didn't mean blowing milkshake around,' Lauren giggled. 'I meant *this*. Getting together after a training session. It's cool, isn't it? We should do it more often.'

I *thought* I heard a muffled beeping, so nervously I took my phone out of my pocket again to check. Of course, it was just my imagination working overtime.

'Ooh, flash phone!' Jasmin commented, noticing it for the first time. 'Is it new?'

'Yes, I got it this morning for my birthday,' I replied distractedly, replacing it in my pocket.

'Hannah, it's your birthday, and you never even said!' Georgie exclaimed.

'Birthday bumps!' Lauren yelled, draining the dregs of her milkshake and jumping to her feet. 'It has to be done!'

'No, really, it's fine—' I began.

No one listened. They hustled me outside and

onto the patch of grass near the car park. Believe me, after what had happened this morning, I'd never felt less like the birthday bumps in my life.

'Katy and Grace – the legs!' Georgie shouted, 'Me and Lauren – the shoulders! And, Jasmin, just grab on to anything else!'

'Wait!' I shrieked, as they tried to upend me. 'My phone!'

I took my mobile out of my pocket and placed it carefully on top of my sports bag. Then I was seized from all angles and unceremoniously turned onto my back. I couldn't help laughing, despite how I was feeling.

'Here we go!' Georgie announced, gripping me tightly. '*One!*'

I flew up into the air and back down and up again so fast, I could hardly laugh and breathe at the same time. I just hoped they didn't drop me!

At the twelfth bump, I was deposited on my back on the grass and I lay there, hiccupping and giggling and trying to catch my breath. The others grinned down at me.

'I *so* can't wait until your birthdays,' I said weakly. 'I shall have my revenge!'

Then I heard a sound from the direction of my

sports bag. My phone was ringing.

I stopped laughing instantly. Shaking, I dashed over to my phone and snatched it up. The display screen said, *Mum calling*.

Gulping, I turned my back on the others so that they couldn't see my face and pressed the *answer* key.

'H-hello, Mum?' I had to clear my throat because my voice wouldn't work properly.

'Hannah, you haven't heard from Olivia, have you?' Mum said immediately. My knees almost went from under me. I could tell from the way she spoke that something was badly wrong.

For a moment, I didn't know how to reply.

'Er – why do you ask?' That seemed the best option until I found out exactly what was going on. After all, there was still a chance that this was nothing to do with the text, although I doubted it.

At the other end of the line, I heard Mum sigh.

'Hannah, you know how upset Olivia was this morning? Well, we think she may have run away from home...'

I bet you can guess *exactly* how I felt right at that moment.

'*What*!' I shrieked, almost falling over with shock. Olivia, the drama queen, had absolutely and totally surpassed herself this time. 'Are you sure? How do you know?'

There was a crackly pause in our conversation while I waited impatiently for Mum to reply.

'Sorry, love,' she said after a moment or two, 'I'm on the hands-free in the car on my way to pick you up, and I couldn't hear that—'

'How do you *know* Olivia's run away?' I repeated.

'Well, Carol says one of their suitcases is missing, and quite a lot of Olivia's clothes are gone. Oh, damn, red light.' I heard a screech as Mum hit the brakes. 'Your dad's beside himself with worry.'

I began pacing up and down, the phone clamped to my ear. I was angry and a bit tearful. I didn't believe it. I *wouldn't* believe it. Oh sure, maybe Olivia *had* packed a suitcase and taken off, all right, but she'd be holed up somewhere nice and warm and safe, like a mate's house. This was a girl who had a panic attack if she broke a nail. There was no way she'd be out on the streets. That probably makes me sound like a hard-faced cow. I'm not. I just know Olivia.

Besides, I was in no mood to be nice about her after getting that horrible text message. And how did *that* fit into all *this*? Knowing Olivia, there had to be an explanation.

'Hannie, I'll be there in about ten minutes,' Mum went on. 'And look, love, Dad's asked me if we could drive around town and look for Olivia. You don't mind, do you?'

'No,' I replied. Well, what could I say? This was turning out to be my most memorable birthday *ever*, for all the wrong reasons.

'Thanks, sweetie. See you very soon.'

I clicked my phone off and turned round. Five pairs of eyes were glued to me, all wide with interest, although Grace and Katy were being polite and trying to pretend they weren't dying of curiosity like the others.

'Are you all right, Hannah?' Grace asked kindly.

I shook my head. 'Not really,' I said in a shaky voice. 'My half-sister Olivia has run away from home.'

'That's terrible!' Lauren gasped. To my surprise, she rushed over and threw her arms around me. 'And on your birthday too. That's the deepest, darkest mega-*pits*, Hannah.'

'I know,' I said in a muffled voice as Lauren smothered me in a bear hug.

The others gathered around me supportively, and I was glad they were there.

'Where do you think she's gone?' Jasmin asked.

'Do you think she'll be OK?' said Katy in a concerned voice.

'Olivia's always OK,' I muttered. 'She only ever looks out for Number One—' I stopped abruptly, realising how super-spiteful that made me sound. 'I mean, I *would* be worried if I thought she'd *really* run away, but I think Olivia's only pretending so that Dad'll do what she wants. He *always* gives in because she's his favourite—'

My voice began to wobble and my eyes began to tear up, so I stopped right there.

'Do you think—' Jasmin began, but broke off with a frown as a red car drove through the car-park gates. 'Oh, *bum*, here comes my mother to pick me up. I don't like to leave you like this, Hannah.'

'Don't worry,' I assured her, although I felt warmed by the other girls' obvious anxiety for me. 'That's my mum in the car behind, so I'll have to go anyway.'

'Look, let us know what happens, yeah?' Georgie said, giving me a gentle punch on the shoulder which I guessed was a Georgie equivalent of

Lauren's bear hug. 'You've got our numbers.'

'OK,' I said quickly. Mum had rolled to a halt and was tooting the horn impatiently.

'Take care,' Lauren yelled as I scooted off across the car park.

'Hope everything turns out OK,' added Jasmin.

I turned back to wave at them and then jumped into the passenger seat.

'Sorry, sweetheart.' Mum was looking pale and harassed. 'I didn't want to drag you away from your friends, but—'

'Mum, it's OK,' I interrupted. 'Has anyone seen Olivia since Dad and I dropped her off this morning?'

Pulling out of the car park, Mum shook her head. 'Carol had already gone shopping by then. No one's seen her.'

'She could be at a mate's house,' I suggested diffidently.

Mum threw me a sharp-eyed glance as she U-turned and headed swiftly out of the car park again. 'I know what you're thinking, Hannie,' she said, 'because I'm thinking exactly the same thing myself. But we don't know for sure that Olivia has done this just for dramatic effect, so we have to treat it seriously in case she really *has* run away. Do you see that?'

I nodded. Now I felt incredibly guilty for being so mean. 'Have you called the police?'

'Your dad and Carol are at the police station now,' Mum replied with a sigh. 'I suppose we'd better go and search for Olivia. It's a long shot, but your dad feels so helpless, I said we would, just to please him.'

'We could try the Millbank shopping centre,' I suggested. 'Olivia and her friends hang out there a lot.'

'Good thinking, honey.' Mum swung the car round, probably illegally, I realised, and we headed off in the opposite direction towards the Millbank.

We parked in the multi-storey car park at the shopping centre and spent the next couple of hours wandering around Topshop, Jane Norman, River Island and every other shop that Olivia might have set foot in. But there was no sign of her. I never really thought there would be.

The texts started coming as we fought our way through the crowds in Topshop.

are u ok han? (Grace)

hve u found O yet? (Georgie)

r u still coming to training 2moz if Ol not back? (Lauren)

hope u r ok hannah! (Katy)

thinking of u and a smiley face (Jasmin)

So there was at least *one* good thing that had happened on my birthday, I thought as Mum and I drove home from the shopping centre in silence. It was still early days, but it looked like I *might* have made five new friends.

'I can't get hold of your dad,' Mum muttered anxiously, trying to make a phone call with one hand and unlock the front door with the other. 'It keeps going to voicemail. Maybe he's left us a message on the answerphone.'

But there were no messages from Dad or anyone else. Now I was starting to get worried. *I could have been a bit nicer to Olivia*, I thought anxiously. Maybe she *was* having problems with her mum, and that's why she wanted to move out. The trouble was, I automatically thought that anything Olivia did, she did to get at me and wind me up. That was the way it had always been.

'It's almost three.' Mum glanced distractedly at the clock, after she'd tried ringing all Olivia's mates again. 'I suppose we ought to have some lunch, although God knows, I don't feel much like eating. Hannah, what time did you say Chloe and Danni were coming over?'

'Five o'clock,' I replied. I could guess what was coming.

'Sorry, hon, I think you're going to have to cancel,' Mum said gently.

I nodded without arguing. I definitely wasn't in the mood for my birthday sleepover anyway.

I tried Chloe and Danni's mobiles but I couldn't get through to either of them. I left voicemail messages, and then, just to be on the safe side, I rang their homes and left more messages with their parents. This simple task left me exhausted, for some reason, and, yawning, I sat down at the kitchen table with Mum, where we both chewed unenthusiastically on cheese sandwiches.

'I think I'll try your dad again,' Mum said, throwing down her sandwich after just a couple of bites. She picked up her phone and hit speed dial. But right at that moment we heard the front door open. There were voices.

Straightaway Mum and I jumped to our feet. We both bolted for the kitchen door but it was opened from the hall before we reached it.

There stood Dad and Olivia in the doorway.

'Panic over!' Dad said, literally beaming from ear to ear. 'Carol and I found her in Silver Beech Park after we'd been to the police station.'

I stared at Olivia. She was looking very solemn and a bit sheepish, but was I the only one who could see a hint of triumph under the *butter wouldn't melt in my mouth, honestly* exterior?

'Sorry, Louise,' Olivia said quietly to my mum. She hung her head, her dark hair falling forward and covering her face. 'I just wanted to get away for a bit and sort my head out. I didn't mean to make everyone worry.'

'It's good to have you back,' Mum said, and gave her a hug.

'I've spoken to Carol and Olivia's going to be staying with us for a few days,' Dad said. Now I could see Olivia's shiny pink suitcase behind them in the hallway. 'Just so that we can let everything settle down and get back to normal. Then we can talk about what's going to happen next.'

'Fine,' Mum agreed, as I stood silently by. I was imagining what would have happened if *I'd* tried to run away from home because I wasn't allowed to do exactly what I wanted. I'd have been grounded in my bedroom with no TV, DVD player or computer until I was thirty-five, at least.

I searched Olivia's face, trying to find any signs of guilty knowledge about that horrible text she'd sent me. But Olivia looked as serene and innocent as an angel. *Yeah, right.*

'Good, well that's all settled, then,' Dad said cheerfully. 'Right, Hannie, shall we order your birthday pizzas before Chloe and Danni get here, or shall we wait till they arrive?'

'Mum told me to cancel the sleepover,' I mumbled. I suppose I could have tried to get hold of Chloe and Danni again and invite them round, but, to be honest, I just didn't feel like it. I was surer than ever that, one way or another, Olivia was going to use my secret to blackmail me into persuading Dad to allow her to stay permanently. So I was going to have *that* hanging over me for the next few days.

'Oh, sorry, Hannah,' said Olivia. To be fair (and believe me, I don't want to be) she *did* sound sorry. Well, a bit.

'We'll all go out for dinner, then,' Dad announced quickly. 'How does that sound?'

'Great!' Olivia linked arms with Dad and flashed

him a dazzling smile. 'But I think Hannah should choose where we go, because it's *her* birthday.'

How generous. But then why *wouldn't* Olivia be generous? She'd got her own way, and even if she was only moving in temporarily to start with, I knew she'd get around Dad in the end.

'Fantastic.' I tried to sound upbeat. 'I'll just go and change.'

I escaped. Upstairs, I flung myself on my bed and buried my face in the pillow. If Olivia *was* moving in for ever, I'd just have to get used to it. Maybe Dad would start being stricter with *her*, I thought hopefully. I had a vision of Olivia sitting at our kitchen table doing her homework, and Dad standing over her yelling, 'Olivia! What have I told you about French verbs? The endings are vital! Never take your eye off the page!' while Mum filmed him. I managed a feeble smile.

Then I remembered I still had one good thing left today. My secret birthday card. I'd brought my bag upstairs with me, so I scrambled across the bed, grabbed it and tore open the pink envelope.

The card had a black-and-white photo of a Siamese cat that made me smile. But the message inside made me cry a few happy tears.

Was it wrong to have a secret like this? Maybe. I knew that I couldn't keep things quiet for ever, but I wasn't quite ready to confess my secret to Mum and Dad yet. But it wasn't just *my* secret now, was it? Olivia knew something was going on. All I could do was keep one step ahead of her and wait and see what she was planning.

And, believe me, Olivia *would* be planning something.

CHAPTER
FIVE

'Hannah, are you *sure* you don't mind getting the bus home after the training session today?' Mum said as we pulled up in the football club car park.

'Mum, you've asked me that fifteen times during the journey already,' I replied patiently. 'The answer is still no, I don't mind. I'm a big girl now. I'm twelve years old, remember?'

I'd even managed to be calm, cool and mature the evening before when Dad took us all to the local Italian. I'd chatted with Olivia, laughed at her jokes and shared my garlic bread with her. All very impressive, when what I *really* wanted to do was tip my bowl of spaghetti Bolognese over her head and scream, *Why did you send me that text?*

'I know.' Mum reached across and smoothed my hair. 'Thanks, Hannie. Dad and I simply can't miss this business meeting this morning. Have a good one, honey. It looked like you were getting on really well with the others yesterday when I picked you up.'

'I was.' Before we went out for dinner, I had texted Grace, Jasmin, Katy, Lauren and Georgie to let them know that Olivia had been found safe and sound, and I was still feeling all warm and marshmallowy inside after the way they'd rallied round me yesterday. A sudden thought struck me.

'Mum, we went for milkshakes yesterday when the training session finished early,' I said, opening the car door. 'If we do that again, is it OK if I stay?'

'Sure thing,' Mum agreed. 'Just text or ring and let me know when you'll be home, all right?'

I jumped out and banged the door shut. As I waved Mum off, Georgie sauntered through the gates.

'Hiya,' I called. 'So the bus didn't break down this morning and your brother didn't hide your football boots?'

'Nope,' Georgie replied, her face splitting into a huge grin. 'But I got my own back. I put Luke's phone in a plastic bag and buried it in the back garden. Now he's going mental because he has all these girls' numbers on there.'

'Has Luke got loads of girls after him, then?' I asked curiously.

Georgie nodded. 'Don't ask me why,' she said with a shrug. 'It's one of the world's great unsolved mysteries.'

We were wandering towards the club entrance as we chatted. Suddenly, behind us, we heard the loud, throaty purr of a car turning in at the gates.

I could just *tell* that it was going to be an expensive car, even before Georgie and I turned to look. And it *was*. It was a long, sleek, black beast of a sports car that seemed to go on for ever. The top was down, and Lauren was sitting in the passenger seat next to a woman who looked like a film star, no lie. The car number plate was *BELL 1*.

'Georgie! Hannah!' Lauren bounced up and down in her seat (cream leather with black trim), waving madly. 'Wait for me!'

The film-star woman pushed her dark shades up on top of her shiny blonde hair as Lauren reached across to kiss her cheek. And I realised with something of a shock that this must be Lauren's mum. I'd never seen her at any of the games since I'd joined the club a few weeks before, although Lauren's dad had been there a couple of times. Lauren often got lifts to and from training sessions and matches with one of the other girls.

''Bye, Mum.' Lauren scrambled out of the car and rushed over to us. 'Hi, guys.'

Georgie raised one dark eyebrow as Mrs Bell swung the car round and headed off. 'Your mum got fed up with the 4x4, then?' she remarked. 'I thought she only bought it a few months ago.'

Lauren shrugged. 'My mum just likes buying new cars,' she explained, looking a bit sheepish.

'Ooh, get her!' Georgie said in a super-sarcastic tone that made even *me* blink a bit. 'You two should both come with me on the bus sometime, try slumming it down with the poor people.'

Lauren flushed. 'Oh, excuse me, I didn't realise it was *my* fault that you have to get the bus,' she said cuttingly, hands on hips. 'I'm *sooo* sorry my parents have got lots of money. Shall I get down on my knees and *beg* you to forgive me?'

'We're late,' I broke in quickly as Georgie and

Lauren angrily stared each other out, nose to nose. Well, they *would* have been if Georgie hadn't towered over Lauren by about ten centimetres. 'I'm going to the changing-room.' I'd seen enough of their quick tempers on the football field to want to keep well out of it.

I dashed off. I could hear from the banging doors behind me that Georgie and Lauren were following me along the corridor, although they weren't saying a word to each other. They quite often argued hotly during matches, though, and it always blew over, so I was pretty sure this would be no exception.

Grace, Jasmin and Katy were already in the changing-room, half-dressed. I went over to them.

'Great that Olivia's back, isn't it?' Jasmin said cheerfully, removing her black and pink lacy top. 'Well, sort of great, I suppose. Actually, it's not great for you at all, is it, Hannah? Sorry.'

I had to smile.

'What's going on with those two?' Grace asked, as Georgie and Lauren tried to push their way into the changing-room at the same time. The doorway wasn't big enough for them both and they jostled each other, with red-faced determination, for a moment, until Georgie finally won by pushing

Lauren aside with her sports bag.

'Georgie was having a go about Lauren's mum's car,' I muttered as Georgie stomped over to us, Lauren scuttling along behind.

'*Another* new one?' Grace winked at me, pulling her long sleek hair into a ponytail.

'They'll be the best of friends again by the end of training,' Katy predicted, undoing her watch and laying it on the bench.

'I'll make them laugh,' Jasmin said in a low voice. 'Just watch.'

As Georgie and Lauren joined us, throwing looks that could kill at each other, Jasmin waltzed over to them.

'Hey, you two, do you think I'd be any good at ballet?' Jasmin asked loudly, her petite frame turning a clumsy pirouette.

Grace, Katy and I tried not to laugh as Georgie and Lauren stared at Jasmin in utter amazement.

'*Ballet?*' Lauren repeated. 'Jasmin, are you raving bananas?'

'Not at all.' Jasmin lifted herself up onto her toes and tottered unsteadily across the changing-room, arms in the air. The other girls who were changing watched in open-mouthed astonishment as Jasmin attempted an acrobatic leap that started badly and ended worse. Some of them started giggling. 'My friend Layla asked me if I wanted to go to a beginner's ballet class with her. I've always fancied dancing the Dying Swan.'

'Don't you mean the Dying Duck?' Georgie enquired.

Jasmin began awkwardly high-kicking her way back across the changing-room towards us, and this time we all laughed, even Georgie and Lauren.

'I think I'm a natural,' Jasmin declared, flinging one of her legs out behind her. Her foot hit the bench and she shrieked. 'Oops!'

Something clattered to the floor.

'Mind my watch!' Katy cried, springing forward.

Off-balance, Jasmin couldn't stop herself from stepping back. We heard a *crack* as she trod squarely on the watch and broke the glass.

'Oh, bum, Katy, I'm *sooo* sorry!' Jasmin yelped, looking absolutely devastated. 'I'm such a twit. But it wasn't like it was *expensive* or anything, was it?'

'*Jasmin*!' Grace whispered fiercely, giving her a shove.

Katy shot Jasmin an angry look, her eyes dark with emotion. 'My dad gave me that watch for my birthday,' she said curtly, her mouth quivering. She bent down and began gathering up the broken pieces, keeping her face turned away from us.

'Maybe it can be fixed,' Jasmin went on anxiously as Katy stood up, still not looking at anyone.

'Jasmin, it's in about a million pieces,' Georgie pointed out bluntly.

Quietly Katy put the broken watch in her locker. Then she went out of the changing-room without a word.

'Oh, I feel so *bad*!' Jasmin wailed. She slumped down onto the bench and stared at us miserably.

'You shouldn't have said that about Katy's watch not being expensive,' Lauren remarked, beginning to change swiftly into her kit. Everyone else had left by now, and we were going to be last again, like yesterday. 'I don't think her family has got a lot of money.'

'Unlike *yours*,' Georgie sniped.

'Don't start that again,' Lauren began.

'Oh, you two can just shut up right now!' Jasmin broke in, her round, pretty face creased in a fearsome frown. 'This is all *your* fault!'

'*Our* fault?' Georgie and Lauren repeated in amazement.

'Yes, Hannah said you'd had a row and I was *trying* to make you laugh,' Jasmin retorted and she stomped out of the changing-room as best as she could in her football boots. Meanwhile Georgie and Lauren both turned to fix me with accusing stares.

'Leave me out of it,' I said, quite sharply for me, but with this Olivia business, I was getting fed up with being pushed around all the time.

'Let's just stop this right now,' Grace cut in firmly. 'We're supposed to be enjoying playing football, not arguing the toss with each other.'

'Oh, the Golden Girl strikes again!' Lauren sighed, rolling her eyes theatrically. 'You're *such* a know-it-all! Do you ever get a break from being so perfect, or is it a full-time job?'

'Yeah, if you're so wonderful, how come you and Gemma don't get along so great?' Georgie demanded.

I was surprised by what I heard. I thought twins *always* got on well together. I didn't think Grace would react to any of this, but to my surprise her face changed and for once, she didn't seem to have an answer. With an angry shrug, she too walked out. Lauren flounced right after her and Georgie followed, pulling up her socks sulkily as she went. Neither of them said another word to each other.

'Oh, great,' I muttered to myself. 'Just *great*.'

What had happened to all that fantastic fun we'd had together yesterday? How had everything gone so wrong? I thought for a moment. I suppose it was then I began to realise that there were a lot of strong personalities among the other five girls. I mean, that was what made them fun and interesting – but it also meant that there was a downside...

Suddenly everything seemed too much for me. Even though I was already late, and Martha was probably going to exterminate me into tiny bits, I grabbed my new phone and dialled a number. It wasn't in my phone book; I'd memorised it. I couldn't risk Mum or Dad finding out who I was calling.

'Hi, it's me,' I said in a low voice, even though there was no one else around. 'Yes, I'm fine. Thanks for the birthday card. Can I come over after training today?'

I grinned as the voice at the other end told me I could, and they'd look forward to it. I rang off, reminding myself that I'd have to be careful, just in case Olivia was on my trail. At that point, Martha appeared, grim-faced, in the doorway.

Well, at least I had something to look forward to

when the training session finished, I thought, feeling a little more cheerful as I struggled to pull on my red boots in record time under Martha's beady eye.

Because you know what? I'd bet my bottom dollar that we wouldn't be going for milkshakes after training today.

CHAPTER SIX

'So how was your football thingy today, Hannah?' Olivia enquired idly. She was lying on the living-room sofa in her white dressing gown, face covered in green gunk and balls of cotton wool between her freshly painted crimson toenails. 'What did you do afterwards?'

'*What?*' I demanded, spinning round and dropping my sports bag with a thump. I'd been looking forward to coming home and slobbing out on the sofa myself, and here was Olivia getting in the way as usual. Mum and Dad were still out, though, so I didn't have to pretend to be nice to her, at least. 'What the hell do *you* want to know *that* for?'

OK, so sue me, but I was in a totally bad mood. The training session had been terrible. None of us were talking to each other much, and Lauren and Georgie were too busy trying to kill each other stone-dead with dirty looks to concentrate on football. Unfortunately (or maybe on purpose) Martha had decided that Lauren and Georgie should partner each other when we were passing in pairs up and down the pitch. They began sneakily trying to trip each other up, and this led to a long and very stern lecture from Martha about working together and getting on with our team-mates during a game even if we *weren't* getting on with them off the pitch.

Did I say I'd made five new friends? What a joke *that* turned out to be. We all got changed as fast as possible in complete silence, and then we headed off immediately after the session, Katy clutching her broken watch. No one even so much as *suggested* milkshakes.

Now here was Olivia sticking the knife in. I wondered nervously if she actually knew where I'd been when training finished, or if she was just fishing to try and discover what my secret was – but, whatever, I was no way going to make it easy for her.

'For God's sake, Hannah, what's up with you?' Olivia sat bolt upright and stared at me, brown eyes hostile. 'Your mum mentioned that you might go out with your team-mates, that's all. I was just being *friendly*. You know, *f-r-i-e-n-d-l-y*. Look it up in the dictionary, sister dear.'

'Half-sister,' I corrected her sulkily. I was determined not to mention the text until I discovered what Olivia was up to. If she could be sneaky and devious, then so could I. And I wouldn't crack first, either. My secret was too important to me for that.

'Oh, like, *whatever*,' Olivia sighed theatrically, rearranging herself more comfortably on the sofa. She didn't offer to move so I could sit down, either. OK, so we have *two* sofas in the living room, but I wanted to sit on *this* one because it's my favourite... God, why does Olivia always bring out the five-year-old in me? 'I don't know why I bothered.'

'Well, I *do*,' I muttered. 'But you're not going to get away with it.'

My half-sister did a perfect impression of someone looking very puzzled and confused. Although it was difficult to tell, really, underneath the sickly green face pack.

'I actually don't have the faintest idea what you're talking about, Hannah,' Olivia informed me in a superior voice that made me itch to shove her off the sofa onto the floor. 'But, hey, if you have any conspiracy theories, why don't you share them with me?'

'Nice try, Olivia,' I snapped. 'That's not going to work either.'

'Oh, I give up.' Olivia shook her head and several blobs of face pack landed on Mum's hand-woven (meaning, expensive) cream rug. 'You're even more of a sad case than I thought, Hannah. OK, so, let's be honest, we hate each others' guts. But we ought to at least *pretend* to get along, if I'm going to be living here—'

'You're not going to be *living* here, Olivia,' I said with a hint of desperation. Well, more a great big dollop of desperation actually. 'Dad said it's only for a few days.'

Olivia smirked. 'We'll see. It's up to Dad, not you, and I know he'd *love* me to move in. He just doesn't want to upset my mum.'

I don't lose my temper very often, but Olivia knows how to press all the right buttons.

'You're right about something,' I said, my voice rising, 'I *do* hate your guts, and I don't want you moving in here and I don't care who knows it.'

'*Hannah*,' said a voice from the doorway.

My heart plunged. It was Dad, and he looked upset and angry. He and Mum must have come in the back way through the conservatory because I hadn't heard the front door open.

'What are you two girls doing?' Dad demanded. 'No, don't answer that,' he went on as Olivia and I both opened our mouths. 'I could hear for myself.' He glanced sternly at me. 'Hannah, apologise to Olivia.'

'But—'

'Now, Hannah.'

I stared down at my feet, not at Olivia. 'Sorry.'

'Hannah, your mum wants a word with you,' Dad said quietly. 'She's in the kitchen. And, Olivia, clean that mess off the rug before Louise sees it.'

'In a minute, Dad, my nails are still wet—'

'No, Olivia, *now*.'

So Olivia wasn't getting off totally scot-free,

I thought with some satisfaction as I stomped off to the kitchen. But it was *me* who'd been made to look like a spoilt, sulky child, even though it was Olivia who'd started it. I just wished Dad could see what Olivia was really like. I was so frustrated, I could *scream. Yes, Hannah, very adult.*

Mum was seated at the kitchen table sorting through a mountain of business paperwork. As I went in, she glanced at me over the top of her specs, her face unsmiling. *Woo-hoo, another telling-off in store, and yet another point to Olivia.*

'I know, I know, Mum,' I burst out, 'you've told me before not to argue with Olivia. But she's *so* flipping smug and know-it-all, she drives me *mad.* And Dad doesn't see it, he just thinks she's so *great*—'

Mum shook her head. 'Hannah, you've got this wrong,' she said. 'Your dad treats you and Olivia equally.'

'He does *not*,' I argued. I couldn't have said these things to Dad – it was hard enough to say them to Mum. But the one thing I had never told anyone, the dark thought that Dad actually loved Olivia more than he loved me, was kept locked away in the back of my mind and left unspoken.

'Hannah, I know Olivia isn't always easy to get on with,' Mum replied, pushing the papers aside. 'But she hasn't had it her own way all her life. You're old enough to see that.'

I was silent. I didn't want to admit that I had no idea what Mum meant, and I didn't want to ask, either. Olivia was Olivia, and that was that. I didn't need to know any more.

'Maybe we should have a talk about this sometime soon,' Mum went on, patting my arm.

'Oh, it'll be OK, Mum.' I shrugged, pretending it was no big deal. Talking about Olivia meant talking about Dad too, and I was scared what might come out. Much better, and safer, to keep quiet. But Mum's not that easy to fool.

'We'll see,' was all she said. 'Anyway, now that things are back to normal – kind of – here, I was wondering if you wanted to have a late birthday sleepover and invite Chloe and Danni to stay on Friday night?'

'Oh, fab, Mum!' I cheered up loads as I headed off to ring my mates. Olivia was on her hands and knees in the living room, scrubbing sulkily at Mum's rug with a wet wipe, I was glad to see, and Dad had taken himself off to his study.

'Hey, Chloe.' Upstairs I stretched out on my turquoise duvet, mobile clamped to my ear. 'It's me. How's you?'

'Oh, hi, Hannah.' Chloe's cheerful, chirpy voice came down the line. 'Gutted, actually, that we missed a *major* pizza pig-out yesterday, because of your half-sister from hell. So's Danni.'

'I know, sorry about that,' I replied with a sigh. 'Anyway, Mum said you could come over on Friday. Let's just hope that *The Evil Half-sister from Planet Me, Me, Me* goes out with her rancid mates. The aliens in *Doctor Who* have got nothing on that lot.'

Chloe roared with laughter. 'You pretend to be so quiet, but you're deadly, really, Han! Can't do Friday though. We're going away this afternoon until Sunday. Last-minute decision by my wonderful parents – we're going to stay in a caravan in the middle of nowhere, would you believe? Hello, bored daughter on the loose! And, anyway, Danni was muttering something about having to visit her gran on Friday evening, so she can't come either.'

'Oh, well, never mind,' I sighed. I'd been looking forward to having some back-up from my mates against Olivia. But maybe she'd be gone by Friday, anyway. *Some hope.*

'How about we go bowling instead next week?' Chloe suggested.

'Excellent idea!' I agreed, perking up again. 'I'll give Dan a call.'

I *did* have some good mates, I reflected, as Chloe rang off. But a girl can always do with more, right? It was just a shame that perhaps Lauren, Georgie, Katy, Jasmin and Grace didn't feel the same way.

'Oh, look, there are the other girls from your team,' Mum remarked innocently as we pulled into the car park the following morning. Jasmin was getting out of her mum's car, and Georgie was with her. They must have stopped to give Georgie a lift, so at least *those* two were talking again. At that moment, Grace also walked through the gates, so all four of us met on the steps up to reception.

'Sorry!' Jasmin said immediately. She flung her arms first around me and then around Grace, hugging us tightly. 'Yesterday was a bit intense, wasn't it? Anyway, we gave Georgie a lift today and she apologised and said that everything was all her fault and she's *really* sorry and can we please forgive her?'

'Jasmin, I never said all that!' Georgie protested,

but I was relieved to see she was smiling. 'OK, I admit I was a bit mean to Lauren yesterday. Sorry.'

'Me too,' Grace said quickly. 'I know I can be a bit bossy. Someone just tell me to shut up and mind my own business in future.'

'I'm sorry as well,' I added.

'What for, Hannah?' Jasmin turned to me, her eyes wide with surprise. '*You* didn't do anything mean yesterday.'

'I know, but I didn't want to be left out of the group hug,' I said with a grin.

'Ooh, yes, group hug!' Jasmin squealed, her brown eyes alight with excitement. 'But we ought to wait for Lauren and Katy—'

There was a loud bang from the street outside, and we all jumped.

'They got me!' I groaned, slumping against Jasmin, and the others giggled.

Next second a little red car turned into the car park, its exhaust backfiring again as it bumped to a halt. We couldn't believe it when we saw Lauren peering at us through the dirty window.

'That *can't* be one of Lauren's mum's cars!' Grace said, her mouth falling open in disbelief. 'No, that's not her mum driving.'

The driver of the car was grey-haired and definitely not the same woman from yesterday. As we all stared, Lauren tumbled out of the car and rushed over to us.

'Oh, absolutely fan-brill-tastic, we're talking to each other again!' she crowed as the little red car chugged away. 'I thought it was going to be all doom and gloom and misery today.'

'Nah, that's Martha's job,' said Jasmin.

Lauren and Georgie looked at each other.

'Sorry,' they both said at exactly the same moment.

'So,' Georgie went on, perfectly straight-faced, 'You must have gone to a lot of trouble to make sure you turned up in a tiny, not-very-posh car this morning. Has your mum sold the sports car and bought that skanky old red one just to make me feel better?'

I wondered a bit nervously if Lauren was going to take offence again, but she simply burst out laughing.

'God, no, that's not ours,' she explained. 'It belongs to our housekeeper, Mrs Melvyn. Mum asked her to drop me off today because she had to go into work early, and Dad's in Germany on business.'

The look on Georgie's face was priceless. '*Housekeeper?*' she spluttered.

'Better go in or we'll be late,' Grace said smoothly. She headed for the revolving doors, skilfully hustling an open-mouthed Georgie along with her.

We all followed, but I noticed that Jasmin was hanging back and kept turning to glance behind her as we went down the corridor.

'What's biting you, Jasmin?' Lauren asked curiously. 'You're all antsy.'

'I'm just looking for Katy,' Jasmin replied, looking a bit sheepish. 'I bought her *this*.'

She fished in her coat pocket and brought out a sparkly pink box etched with silver stars. As we gathered round, she flipped it open. Inside was a pretty watch with a round, pearly face and a plaited pink-leather strap.

'Ooh, cute!' said Lauren.

'I took some money out of my savings account to buy it,' Jasmin confided. 'I hope the wrinklies don't find out because they will seriously kill me. I'm supposed to be saving my pocket money for our trip to India next Christmas.' She looked anxiously at us. 'D'you think Katy'll like it?'

'She'll love it,' Grace replied firmly, and the rest of

us nodded. Secretly I thought the watch looked more like something that Jasmin would wear herself. It wasn't really Katy's style at all. Her broken watch had been very simple, a square face with a brown strap. But it was the thought that counted. I just hoped Katy would appreciate Jasmin's thoughtful gesture. Trouble was, Katy was so quiet and reserved, you never quite knew how she would react...

When we reached the changing-room, Jasmin looked around eagerly but Katy wasn't there. Jasmin's face fell. Fifteen minutes later we were out on the pitch warming up, and Katy still hadn't arrived.

'This is all my fault,' Jasmin wailed, as we sprinted in formation towards lines of cones and then back again. 'Katy's not coming today. Oh!' She stopped suddenly and Lauren careered heavily into the back of her. 'I've just thought – what if Katy doesn't come back at all? What if she's left the team?'

'What if my nose is broken?' Lauren groaned, rubbing her face.

'Jasmin, keep moving!' Martha roared.

'Freya's going to be *really* furious with me if

Katy's left the Springhill Stars,' Jasmin fretted as we practised running, stopping and turning with the ball. We were all standing in two long lines, facing each other, and Jasmin was next to me. 'She's always saying what a fab player Katy is. Maybe Freya will be so angry, she'll throw *me* out of the team.'

When it was my go, I dribbled my football forward, ready to change balls with Georgie, who was opposite me in the other line. Georgie and I swapped over, and as I turned to dribble back to my place as fast as I could, I saw Katy coming up the players' tunnel.

'I think you're off the hook, Jasmin,' I whispered.

Jasmin's face lit up as she saw Katy go over to Mike. Katy spoke quietly to him, and he nodded. I suppose she was apologising for being late. Then, without any fuss and ignoring Martha's black look, Katy came over and joined the end of our line. She smiled warmly at me and Jasmin, and I heard Jasmin sigh with relief.

After that the training session went brilliantly, and time flew past. We played a game that was a real laugh. We all stood on the start line while Martha and Mike placed the balls about six metres away from us. When Mike blew his whistle, we had to charge forward and grab a ball. The thing was, there was one less ball than there were girls, so someone was always left without one. That girl then had to try to get a ball from someone else by tackling them, while we all tried to get back to the start line and keep our own ball safe. It was screamingly funny, especially when Georgie was left without a ball and dashed around like a mad thing, trying to get one. I was 'It' twice, and both times I managed to nick a football for myself, one from Lauren and one from a girl called Sophie. It was amazing, I thought, how much better I was at tackling without Dad yelling at me all the time.

'Oh, that was massive fun,' Lauren sighed as, wet, muddy and messy, we tramped off the pitch at the end of the session. It had started to drizzle with rain at some point, but we were having such a laugh we hadn't even noticed.

'Anyone staying for milkshakes today?' Georgie asked as we pulled off our kits in the changing-room.

Jasmin shook her head. 'I can't,' she said. 'I've got to run. Mum's picking me up, and we're going shopping.'

'Me neither,' Lauren chimed in, kicking off her

gold boots. 'Mum said I had to be ready on time today.'

'Yeah, mustn't keep the housekeeper waiting,' Georgie said with a sly grin, and Lauren gave her a friendly shove.

'I've got to go too.' Katy was already in her clothes and brushing out her straight dark hair. 'I have to look after my little brother while my mum goes to work.'

Grace, Lauren, Georgie and I glanced pointedly at Jasmin. Looking very nervous, Jasmin rooted in her jacket pocket and pulled out the watch.

'Katy, I was really and truly sorry about breaking your watch yesterday,' Jasmin said solemnly. 'So I bought you this.'

She held out the pink box. Katy stared at it as if it was a stick of dynamite.

'What is it?' she asked, not smiling.

'Open it and see,' Jasmin urged.

We all stood there in silence as reluctantly Katy took the box and flicked it open. She looked down at the watch and still her face didn't change. Lauren nudged me discreetly and raised her eyebrows at me. I could see she was as tense as I was. I wondered if Katy was secretly embarrassed because she didn't want to be seen as a charity case. It was obvious that her family had much less money than any of ours did.

'Don't you like it?' Jasmin asked, sounding disappointed.

'It's very pretty,' Katy said quietly. 'But I can't take it, Jasmin. If I want a new watch, I can buy one myself, you know.'

'Oh, but you *have* to keep it!' Jasmin implored, her eyes wide as Katy held the box out to her. 'It was my fault your watch got broken. *Pleeeeze* let me replace it or I'll never forgive myself for the rest of my life, not ever.'

'No pressure, then, Jasmin,' Georgie remarked, trying to lighten the heavy atmosphere a bit.

'Oh, go on, Katy,' Grace said cheerfully, 'take the watch. Otherwise we might have to threaten you with another of Jasmin's ballet routines.'

'Yes, excellent idea,' Jasmin agreed. 'I shall perform the dance of the Sugar-Bum Fairy, unless you take it.' She grinned her sweet and ditsy smile. 'Please? Pretty, pretty please?'

At last Katy smiled too, and I think we all let out a sigh of relief. I know I did. 'Well, thank you,' she said. 'It's lovely.' She took the watch carefully out of the box and strapped it onto her wrist. 'But you didn't have to, Jasmin.'

'I know I didn't *have* to,' Jasmin replied cheerfully, 'I *wanted* to. That's the difference.'

'I'm s-o-o-o glad that's sorted out.' Lauren began stuffing her kit into her sports bag. 'But now I'm later than someone who is *very* late indeed. Maybe we can do the milkshake thing after training tomorrow?'

'Actually, I was thinking we could get together on Friday evening after our last training session,' Grace suggested. 'I know we've got the match to finish off the course on Saturday, but maybe we could have a girlie night in at someone's house with DVDs and stuff?'

'I have a fabulous idea,' Georgie announced, grinning broadly. 'I'm so clever, I amaze myself sometimes.'

'Sorry, Georgie, I don't have the time to argue right now,' Lauren sniggered, picking up her bag. 'But can I just say that I *officially* disagree with that last remark.'

Georgie ignored her. 'Hannah's,' she said, spinning round and pointing a finger at me. I immediately felt guilty, although I had no idea why!

'Hannah's what?' Jasmin asked, giggling.

'Remember Hannah had to cancel her birthday sleepover with her mates because Olivia went missing?' Georgie went on. 'Well, why don't *we* have a sleepover at Hannah's on Friday night? We can all bring some sweets and chocolate and have a late birthday choc-fest!'

'Cool idea,' Lauren agreed, heading for the door. 'I'm in.'

'Me too,' Jasmin declared.

Grace turned to me. 'Does that sound good to you, Hannah?' she asked.

HELP!!!

CHAPTER SEVEN

'I – er – yeah, OK,' I finally managed. 'It sounds great. I'll have to ask my mum and dad, though.'

Look, I liked the other girls. I did, I really did. They were all funny and sweet and kind and interesting, in their own ways. But put us all together and – BAM! It seemed to end in fireworks pretty often. Oh well, I thought, trying to see the bright side, it would be an experience to see how Olivia dealt with Georgie, Lauren, Grace, Jasmin and Katy all at once. Georgie on her own could probably eat Olivia for breakfast. The thought cheered me enormously.

'I'm not sure I'll be able to come,' Katy said as we all followed Lauren out of the changing-room. She'd scooted off, though, and was halfway down the corridor by now.

'Why not?' Georgie turned to stare at her. 'You've *got* to come, Katy. It won't be the same without you.'

'Absolutely,' Jasmin agreed. 'We're just like the Three Musketeers. Except there's six of us.'

Katy looked a bit uncomfortable. 'Sorry, Hannah,' she said, 'I'd love to be there, but I might be needed at home.'

'Why?' Jasmin asked inquisitively, only to be elbowed soundly in the ribs by Grace.

I sighed a quiet sigh that only I could hear. It just seemed like we didn't know each other well enough to get together without something monumental (and I do mean *mental*) going on. Oh dear. Well, I supposed it would take my mind off my feud with Olivia at least...

'Ooh, no, that's my phone!' Jasmin groaned, stopping dead in the middle of the corridor as a burst of Bollywood film music echoed around us. '*Why* does someone always send me a text when my phone's in the bottom of my bag?'

'You *have* to come to Hannah's, Katy,' Georgie declared as we went on to reception, leaving Jasmin kneeling down, rooting frantically through her things. 'As your goalkeeper, I command it.'

Katy didn't answer. We all went over to Lauren, who was waiting by the glass revolving doors, peering outside.

'Typical,' Lauren said grumpily, scanning the car park, 'Mrs Melvyn isn't here to pick me up yet.'

'You just can't get the staff these days, can you?' Georgie remarked. 'We're trying to persuade Katy that she has to come on Friday.'

'Oh, *'course* you have to be there, Katy,' Lauren said. 'It won't be the same without you.'

Katy shrugged. 'We'll see,' she replied calmly. 'Bye.' And she slipped out through the revolving doors before Georgie or anyone else could say another word. Secretly I admired Katy for being able to stand up for herself like that.

'Well, how d'you like that?' Georgie said, staring after Katy as she hurried across the car park. 'Doesn't that girl know how to have any *fun*?'

'We've never seen any of Katy's family at our matches, remember?' Grace pointed out as we stood aside to let a boy with a sports bag come in through the revolving doors. 'Maybe she has problems at home.'

Which was *exactly* what I wanted to say, but I was a teensy-weensy bit scared of Georgie's reaction.

Georgie looked slightly ashamed of herself.

'I know, but she needs to chill a bit—'

'Maybe Katy feels awkward,' I suggested, plunging right in there. 'She might not have the money to do all the stuff we do.'

I glanced at Grace for support, but she wasn't listening. She was looking at the boy with the sports bag, who was about fifteen with blue eyes and a spiky dark crop, and he was looking at her, too. Even though Grace was only wearing a denim mini-skirt and a simple white T-shirt, she did look stunning. I saw the boy give her a half-smile and a wink. Grace blushed.

'Ooh, see that?' Lauren burst into a fit of giggles. 'That boy fancies Grace!'

'Lauren, do you have to be so stupendously childish?' Grace asked, sticking her nose in the air, her long blonde hair swishing.

'No, of course I don't *have* to be, but it's lots of fun,' Lauren retorted smartly. 'He winked at you!'

'He did not,' Grace snapped, trying not to blush even pinker.

'Well, he had a very twitchy eye then,' Lauren said with a gurgle of laughter. 'Can we come to the wedding?'

'Oh, *please*!' Grace flounced into one of the revolving compartments and Lauren stepped in after her, singing 'Here Comes the Bride'. Georgie and I got into the one behind them.

Suddenly Jasmin rushed up to the doors.

'Sorry!' she gasped, 'I couldn't find my phone for ages, and then it was just some really stupid text!'

'Jasmin, there isn't room for you!' I said, alarmed, as she began squeezing in with me and Georgie.

'I'm in now!' Jasmin yelled.

We were jammed in like sardines in a very small tin. We whizzed round, and when our compartment reached the outside, Georgie and I flew out like champagne corks from a bottle. Jasmin wasn't able to get out fast enough, though.

'Help!' she shrieked, whizzing round again on her own, her small figure a blur behind the glass. 'Get me out!'

'The revolving doors are not a *toy*,' the receptionist called sternly from her desk.

This time Jasmin managed to tumble out, red-faced, to join the rest of us. Looking flustered, she skidded on the rubber doormat and almost went head-first down the steps. Lauren managed to catch her arm and hold her – I don't quite know how, though, because we all were laughing like drains.

But at the same time I was thinking, *What the hell have I let myself in for?*

'So, you crazy lot,' Georgia announced, 'what are we going to do to make Hannah's birthday sleepover the most unforgettable she's ever had?'

I was tempted to say, *Just turn up and something's bound to happen*, but I thought that might be a bit mean, so I kept quiet. I didn't think I was ever going to forget this sleepover, anyway.

'I dunno yet, but I'll think of something,' Lauren replied, winking at me. 'Here's Mrs Melvyn. Bye, y'all, have a nice day!' she added in a fantastically authentic American accent, and then she bounced off down the steps.

'You look a bit worried, Hannah,' Grace said with a grin as we followed Lauren into the car park. 'We'll keep Lauren under control, don't worry.'

'Oh no, it's fine,' I said quickly, not wanting to

look like a completely weak and feeble softie. 'I'm sure the sleepover'll be fun.'

'Try not to wince when you say that, Hannah,' Georgie advised me with an amused smirk. 'We might believe you, then.'

'Georgie, do you want a lift?' Grace asked, waving at a blonde woman waiting in a silver car. 'We can go your way.'

'Excellent,' Georgie agreed. 'See you tomorrow, Hannah.'

'Yep, see you, Han!' Jasmin grinned at me as she ran over to meet her mum.

I waited on the steps, waving as they all drove off. I was secretly glad that no one had asked me if Mum or Dad was picking me up because I would have had to lie. If I'd told the truth, that no one was collecting me today, one of the others would have offered me a lift. But I wasn't going straight home. And I didn't want anyone, not even Grace and the others, to know where I was *really* going.

I hung around the car park for five more minutes to make sure it was safe to leave. Then I ducked out of the gates and ran for the bus stop at the end of the road. I'd told Mum I was going to Chloe's after training today. I wasn't used to lying to her and

Dad, though, and my heart was pounding wildly as the bus arrived and I jumped on. I wasn't sure how I'd got away with it so far, I thought as I paid my fare and sat down towards the back of the lower deck. And now my secret was being threatened by Olivia. But I wasn't going to stop. Not yet. Not until I'd decided on the best way to handle all this, anyway...

Fifteen minutes later I was hurrying down the familiar street of terraced houses. I stopped at the house with the blue door halfway along, and rang the bell. A moment later I heard footsteps inside, coming down the hallway.

The door opened.

'Hello, Grandpa,' I said, with a big smile.

Grandpa Fleetwood was my dad's dad. They'd fallen out in a big way before I was born and they hadn't had any contact with each other for more than twenty years, so I'd never met Grandpa until a few months ago. My dad's mum, Grandma Fleetwood, was divorced from Grandpa and she'd gone back to Australia, where she was born. We'd visited her there when I was eight years old, and we kept in touch by email and webcam. My mum's parents, Gramps and Nan Phillips, lived miles away in Scotland and yet we still saw them quite regularly. But Grandpa Fleetwood lived in the same town as us, and yet he was never mentioned. When I was growing up, I kind of knew that I had another grandfather, but I also accepted that we never talked about him. I never asked why. Even when I was a little kid, I just knew it was better not to.

Grandpa's card had arrived last Christmas, and I only found out about it by chance when I overheard Mum and Dad discussing it. I was skulking around outside the kitchen, hoping to get a hint of what they'd bought me for a present – OK, so it was childish, but I *was* only eleven at the time, you know. The door was closed, but I could still hear what they were saying. I didn't mean to listen, honest, but I couldn't help it.

'...and if Dad thinks a Christmas card's going to make things OK between us, then he's wrong,' my dad was exclaiming angrily. 'I've told him before, I don't want *anything* to do with him.'

'I think you're being a bit unreasonable, Matt,' Mum replied calmly. 'Jack's made the first move, so you shouldn't throw it back in his face. Look, he's put his new address and phone number inside the card.'

'Well, we won't be needing *that* information, will we?' Dad had retorted bitterly.

I found the card, I memorised Grandpa's address and then added his phone number to my mobile, deleting that a few days later when I'd managed to memorise it too.

It took until March before I finally managed to find the courage to ring my grandfather in secret. Since then I'd visited him three times and still no one knew. I wondered how long that would last, though, now that Olivia was on my case.

'Hannah!'

I always got a slight shock when I saw Grandpa because he looked so much like my dad, tall and slim and straight with the same direct brown eyes and the exact same chestnut-coloured hair, although Grandpa's is streaked with white.

'I didn't think I'd see you for a while as you popped round yesterday,' Grandpa added.

'I wanted to surprise you,' I said. A Siamese cat appeared, twining its way between Grandpa's ankles, and I bent down, putting my hand out hopefully. 'Hi, Sheba.'

Sheba ignored me and stalked off, tail in the air.

'I think she's getting used to you,' Grandpa said

with a grin. 'Come in, love. I'll put the kettle on.'

As the kettle boiled and Grandpa fed Sheba, I wandered around the small living room. The walls were covered with photos. There were lots of my dad, some in school uniform but most of them on the football field. Grandpa had been a bank manager, but he was also a qualified youth soccer coach, and there were photos of all the teams he'd been involved with, too. I'd seen all the pictures before, but one always drew me back. It was a photo of my dad taken when he was a teenager. His hair is long and wavy, he has a gold earring (I know, how totally embarrassing, but it *was* the 1980s), and he is wearing an Arsenal shirt. Grandpa is standing next to him, they have their arms round each other's shoulders and they are smiling.

I didn't know what had happened to change that, and no one would tell me.

'Mum and Dad OK?' Grandpa asked, carrying in two cups of tea and a plate of ginger biscuits.

I nodded. The first time I visited Grandpa, he'd made it clear that he wouldn't discuss the past and what had happened with Dad. He thought it would be disloyal. So this was all he ever asked.

'And Olivia?'

'She's fine,' I replied, although the words stuck in my throat a bit. I hadn't told Grandpa how I felt about Olivia because they'd never met and I thought it was a bit unfair if I moaned about her before she and Grandpa even got to know each other. Suddenly it struck me how many secrets my family seemed to have, even though we appeared so normal on the outside.

'You know what I'm going to say next, don't you, Hannah?' Grandpa stared questioningly at me with those brown eyes that were just like Dad's. That was probably why I'd felt so comfortable and at ease with him, right from the start.

'Yes, I know.' I tried to smile to hide my anxiety. Grandpa had told me during my very first visit that we couldn't keep this a secret for ever. That sometime very soon we'd have to tell Mum and Dad. I just didn't know *how*.

'It has to be done, you know, love,' Grandpa urged, handing me a cup of tea. 'I can be there with you when you tell them, if you want.' He grinned wryly at me. 'Then they can be angry with both of us.'

I was silent. I didn't know if Grandpa turning up on our doorstep would make things even worse.

I just didn't know what to do, especially as Olivia had found out there was something going on. That made everything much more complicated. I was terrified of telling Dad, so maybe it *would* be easier if Olivia told him before I did. But then, Dad would be absolutely furious that I hadn't owned up myself. I was *so* scared that Dad would stop me seeing Grandpa, though, just when I was starting to get to know him.

'I want to finish the football course first,' I said. 'Then I'll think about it at the end of this week. Promise.' That would buy me some time to decide the best way to work this thing out. Although, like I already told you, I don't think there *was* a best way for me. Olivia was going to come out triumphantly on top, whatever happened.

Grandpa nodded. He didn't say anything more, but I knew he wasn't going to let me off the hook.

'And what happened with the other girls?' he asked, offering me a biscuit. 'Did the fur fly again today, or did you make it all up?'

'Oh, we made up.' I bit into my biscuit as Sheba strolled into the room, giving me a dirty look. 'They're all coming to sleep over at mine on Friday night, if Mum says yes.'

'Hmm.' Grandpa gave me a penetrating look. 'Call me a daft old man, but I get the feeling you're not exactly jumping for joy.'

'No, no, I like them, I do, honestly,' I began. Grandpa raised his eyebrows quizzically at me, and I couldn't help smiling. 'Well, all right, I guess I'm a bit worried about what might happen,' I admitted. 'We have huge fun messing around and stuff, but sometimes—' I remembered what Jasmin had said earlier that morning – 'it gets a bit *intense*.'

Grandpa nodded. 'They're all strong personalities, by the sound of it,' he said. 'That can be a good thing if they're prepared to work hard and put the team first. And I always used to encourage my players to get together away from training. Bonding's a great idea – it improves communication on and off the pitch.'

'You think?' I asked eagerly. Yesterday Grandpa had talked coaching and tactics with me, and I'd *loved* it. He knew so much. We'd kicked a ball around in his back garden and he was direct with me, giving me lots of praise but not afraid to criticise me either. He didn't do it like Dad, though, in a shouty, annoyed way.

'I do.' Grandpa offered me another biscuit. 'And

you'll cope. You're your dad's daughter after all, and he was always a strong character, too. Now tell me what you did at training today…'

I stayed half an hour or so with Grandpa, and then said goodbye. Sheba *almost* let me stroke her without hissing when I left, which was a good sign. I told Grandpa I'd visit again tomorrow. I wanted to see him as much as possible just in case Dad put a stop to my visits when he found out the truth.

And anyway, even if I didn't tell Mum and Dad yet, I knew that once I was back at school, it would be really difficult to make excuses to get away. Mum would be on my case about homework, and then there would be football training twice a week in the evenings and matches on Saturday mornings. My heart sank at the thought of Dad standing on the touchline yelling at me once more…

I felt a lot happier about the sleepover on Friday night, though, as I hurried back to the bus stop. Like Grandpa had said, it would be a good idea to get to know the other girls better. If we got to be *really* good mates, maybe our football would improve.

I stood at the bus stop, daydreaming about winning our league and getting promotion next season, as well as lifting the County Cup. Suddenly a horribly familiar voice cut into my lovely little fantasy.

'Hannah! What are *you* doing here?'

I swear I almost keeled over in horror. There was Olivia coming down the street towards me with Magda, her mate with the multi-coloured hair.

'O-Olivia!' I spluttered, trying not to look guilty.

'Ooh, she does *look* guilty, Olivia,' Magda said, grinning as she peered at me from under her purple fringe. 'What do you reckon she's been up to?'

'Something she's not supposed to be doing, I bet,' Olivia said with a nasty smirk.

'Are you following me?' I blurted out anxiously. It *could* be a coincidence that I'd met Olivia. But it was far more likely that Olivia was on my trail, trying to discover what I was up to. Had she seen me coming out of Grandpa's house?

'Get her!' Olivia nudged Magda. 'Self-important or what?' She narrowed her eyes suspiciously. 'I thought your mum said you were going to Chloe's.'

'So?' I snapped, putting on a show of bravado.

'Well, isn't Chloe the blonde girl who lives near our mate McKenzie?' Olivia pointed out smugly. 'That's *miles* from here.'

I was caught, and I knew I had to get myself out of it fast. *Come on, Hannah.*

'Well, if you must know, Chloe's parents suddenly decided to go away for a few days,' I replied coldly. 'I didn't realise until I got Chloe's text while I was at football, so one of the other girls on the course asked me round hers instead. She lives over there.' And I deliberately pointed in the opposite direction to Grandpa's house. I glanced anxiously at Olivia, but her face didn't change. I don't *think* she'd seen me at Grandpa's. But it had been a close thing.

'I still think it's suspicious, don't you, Liv?' Magda chortled, shaking her pink dreadlocks.

'Absolutely,' Olivia agreed. 'So come on, Han, spill your guts – *have* you got a secret boyfriend? I know it's unlikely, but some people just aren't that fussy and they say there's someone out there for everyone, however weird they are. So there's definitely hope for you yet.'

I glared at Olivia and Magda as they both shrieked with laughter, holding melodramatically on to each other for support.

'Here's my bus,' I said in a dignified manner. 'Goodbye.'

It looked like I might just have got away with it this time, I thought as I left the two giggling idiots behind me and climbed onto the bus. But I knew that Grandpa was right. I couldn't carry on like this. I had to take charge of the situation before Olivia got in first. And that meant confessing to Dad.

To say I wasn't looking forward to it was the understatement of all time.

CHAPTER EIGHT

'A sleepover with your team-mates sounds like a great idea, sweetie.' To my surprise, Mum was really enthusiastic when I cautiously put the idea to her later that day. 'It'll be good to get to know them better, especially if you're going to be visiting them at home.'

'Mum, I've already *said* sorry,' I mumbled. Olivia had, of course, lost no time in letting Mum know that I hadn't been to Chloe's at all and that she'd met me in a different area of town. All part of her plan to annoy me and make me sweat, no doubt. So I'd been forced to use the same cover story about visiting one of the other girls from the team. Mum had started asking me all about it, but luckily the phone rang and she got distracted. I realised, though, that I might have to ask one of the girls to lie for me if Mum carried on with her Sherlock Holmes bit, and that would have meant explaining my secret to Grace or one of the others. I was fairly sure that they'd back me up, but I really didn't want to involve them. Things were spinning out of control, and it was all Olivia's fault. She always messed up *everything*.

'It's OK, Hannie, just let me know where you are next time, hmm?' Mum was in the study, sorting through the business accounts and had one eye on her laptop. 'I know you're sensible, love, but I do worry.'

I nodded, utterly relieved that I seemed to have escaped detection once again. If only there was some way of throwing Olivia off the scent. I'd have to think about that one.

My phone beeped in my pocket. I fished it out and a text message from Lauren popped up.

wanna come 2 footie field in silver beech park @ 4 to have a kick about? L x

'Mum, can I go to the park to meet Lauren?' I asked, showing her the text message.

'No problem, honey, but be back by six, will you?' Mum replied, tapping away at the keyboard. 'Olivia's cooking dinner tonight, and you don't want to miss that.'

'Olivia – cooking?' I pretended to swoon like a Victorian lady and fell backwards into the leather armchair. 'I think I'm hearing things.'

'Your dad and I decided it's about time she started helping out with the chores,' Mum replied with a straight face, but I could see her lips twitching. 'Don't get too excited, it's only pasta and Dolmio sauce.'

'Has Dad said anything about when Olivia's going home?' I asked casually. I'd deliberately bent over to put my trainers on when I said this so that Mum couldn't see my face.

'No, he and Carol are still discussing it.'

'Oh.' It didn't sound like it would be any time soon, I thought gloomily, as I grabbed my denim jacket and left the house.

Silver Beech Park was only about ten minutes' walk from our house. The football fields were behind the playground, on the other side of the park, and as I headed across the grass I saw Georgie standing between the goalposts and Jasmin about to boot the ball at her.

'Hey!' I shouted, waving my arms.

Jasmin looked round, waved and then took a shot at goal. The ball whizzed past Georgie and Jasmin gave a whoop of delight.

'Yay, me!' she shouted.

'Oh, that's *such* a fluke!' Georgie yelled, chasing after the ball, which had gone whizzing off across the grass because there was no net between the posts. 'Come on, Jasmin, best of three.'

I took off my denim jacket and flung it down on the grass, on top of Georgie's black hoodie and Jasmin's pink fleece. Meanwhile, Jasmin placed the ball on the penalty spot and took a short run-up. This time she placed the ball neatly to Georgie's left.

'Woo-hoo! I rock!' Jasmin crowed. She pulled her pale blue sweatshirt over her head and began imitating an aeroplane, running around the pitch with her arms held out, ducking and diving this way and that. Georgie and I giggled.

'There's Grace and Lauren.' Georgie shaded her eyes from the afternoon sun and pointed across the field. Grace looked gorgeous and cool, as always, in skinny jeans and a red hoodie. Lauren, wearing a silvery-grey top and black cut-offs, was bouncing along beside her, waving her hands around and talking animatedly. 'What do you bet that Katy won't come?'

'Get off Katy's case, Georgie,' I said. It came out a bit more sharply than I'd intended, which surprised me and made Georgie's dark eyes open wide. 'She'll come if she can.'

'I bet she doesn't,' Georgie muttered.

'Hey, Katy!' Georgie and I both spun round as we heard Jasmin yelling. 'Over here!'

Katy was running across the grass towards us, a smile on her face. She reached us just as Grace and Lauren did.

'Surprised to see me, Georgie?' Katy asked, her dark eyes twinkling as she threw her cream puffa jacket down on the pile of coats. 'Did you bet that I wouldn't come?'

'She bet her Spurs shirt, actually,' I replied. 'I won, so hand it over, Georgie.'

'You're kidding, Hannah—' Georgie began, looking slightly worried.

'No, I'm not,' I replied, straight-faced. 'We need a new dishcloth.'

Georgie shrugged and pulled a fearsome, cross-eyed face at me while the others grinned.

'What can you expect from a Gooner?' Georgie asked, giving me a friendly shove.

'This is great, isn't it?' Lauren announced, her face split in a huge grin as we divided ourselves into two teams – me, Georgie and Lauren against Grace, Jasmin and Katy. 'I'm glad I thought of it. We ought to do this more often.'

I remembered that this was exactly what Lauren had said when we went for milkshakes and it puzzled me a bit. I know Freya, our coach, was keen for us to get to know each other, but surely Lauren must have *loads* of friends? So why was she always so keen to hang out with all of us? It was a bit of a mystery.

We decided to play a kind of mini-game, three against three. We didn't have goalkeepers because there weren't enough of us, so the only rule was to get as many goals as we could and also to stop the other team from scoring.

'Three-nil!' Jasmin yelped triumphantly as Grace completed her hat-trick with a smooth strike past Lauren, who had rushed between the goalposts to try and stop her.

'Come *on*, guys!' Georgie said, frowning at me and Lauren. She always hated losing, even if it wasn't a real match. 'We need to score!'

'It's Katy,' I panted. 'She never lets us get past her.'

'I'm a defender,' Katy called with a grin. 'That's what I do!'

'Three-nil, three-nil, three-nil, three-nil!' Jasmin chanted, salsa dancing around the pitch. While Katy and Grace were laughing at her, Lauren sneakily retrieved the ball and passed it to Georgie. Georgie thundered towards the opposite goal and belted the ball between them.

'*G-o-o-o-o-o-o-al!*' Georgie shouted, jumping up and down, almost helpless with laughter.

'Ooh, that's so not fair!' Jasmin gasped indignantly. 'We weren't ready!' She and Georgie both pelted over to retrieve the ball, and the rest of us followed.

'It's mine!' Georgie shouted, trying to hook the ball away with her foot.

'Liar, liar, pants on fire!' Jasmin spluttered, grabbing Georgie's T-shirt. 'It's mine! Give it here!'

'Geroff!' Georgie yelled, trying to pull herself free.

'Hey, look at the little girlies giving it handbags at twenty paces!' someone shouted.

I looked round. A couple of teenage boys were standing on the touchline, laughing their stupid heads off. We ignored them. Katy dashed over to Georgie and Jasmin and managed to sweep the ball away from both of them. She passed it to Grace, who immediately turned and ran with her long-legged stride towards our goal.

'Shouldn't you be at home doing your nails, darlin'?' the older boy shouted.

Grace half-glanced up and frowned, which gave me the chance to tackle her and get the ball back. Katy lunged at me, but it was a bit of a clumsy challenge and she stumbled, almost falling flat on her nose, which was totally unlike her. The two boys were laughing helplessly by this stage.

'This is better than a comedy film,' one of them remarked. 'Come on, Georgie, your turn to make a fool of yourself now!'

'Yeah, everyone knows girls are only good for one thing where footie's concerned,' the other added, smirking. 'Better get home and wash our dirty kits, Georgie!'

I stopped with the ball at my feet and glanced uncertainly at Georgie. She *knew* these two idiots?

'Aren't those your brothers, Georgie?' Grace asked.

'Yes, unfortunately.' Georgie was pale with rage. 'Just ignore them. They'll go away.'

'Why are they being so mean?' Katy asked, wide-eyed.

'It's just what boys *do*,' Georgie muttered, looking very uncomfortable. 'I give back as good as I get from Luke and Josh, don't worry.'

'I've only got one brother and that's quite enough,' Katy went on as the two boys strolled off, still laughing. 'Does your mum know they tease you about football like this?'

Georgie suddenly went very still and quiet. 'I don't have a mum,' she replied abruptly, and went to get her jacket.

Katy looked horrified. 'Oh dear, I've said something bad,' she muttered anxiously.

'It's OK, Katy,' Lauren replied, 'Georgie's mum died about three years ago. She had cancer.'

Grace and Jasmin nodded solemnly.

'God, how terrible,' I said with a shiver. Suddenly all my problems with Olivia seemed very unimportant indeed.

'I must say sorry,' Katy murmured, and she immediately went over to Georgie. They spoke together quietly for a few minutes, while the rest of us collected our own jackets. I don't know what Katy said, but Georgie was smiling – sort of – when they both came to join us.

'Don't you think Grace, Katy and I deserve

some sort of reward for beating the pants off you three?' Jasmin enquired as we wandered towards the playground.

Lauren grabbed an empty Diet Coke can that stood on a nearby wall, and held it out to Jasmin.

'Allow me to present you with this magnificent silver trophy in recognition of your wonderful victory,' she said in a posh, plummy Royal Family kind of voice. 'You did very well for common and vulgar peasants.'

'Ta very much, Your Highness,' Jasmin said, taking the 'trophy' with a curtsey. Then she gave a little scream as a wasp appeared from nowhere and buzzed determinedly towards the sticky can. 'Help!'

'Drop the can and keep calm,' Grace advised. Jasmin did drop the can, but she also danced hysterically up and down, waving her arms and trying to swat the wasp away.

'Where's it gone?' Lauren asked.

'It's on Grace's hair!' Georgie shouted.

Grace gave a yell and began shaking her head wildly.

'Keep calm!' Jasmin reminded her, hardly able to get the words out because she was laughing so much.

As we all shot off in different directions to avoid the wasp, I just happened to glance over at the garden on the other side of the playground. There I saw a flash of bright purple that looked familiar and I realised it was Olivia's friend Magda. She was sprawled on the grass and Olivia was sitting next to her. Six of their other mates were there too.

I took a few steps across the playground, keeping out of sight behind the Super Slide so that they didn't notice me. Was that *smoke* I could see?

'I think we finally defeated the wasp, Han.' Lauren came to stand next to me. 'What *are* you doing?'

'Ssh!' I hissed. 'Keep quiet and act natural!'

'How is lurking behind a slide and spying on people acting natural?' Lauren asked, as the others joined us.

'Is this some kind of game?' Jasmin giggled.

'Look!' I whispered, 'That's my half-sister, Olivia, in the garden. The girl in the black jacket.'

'Really!' Grace exclaimed, and they all peered at Olivia with interest.

'At least she isn't the scary one with the pink hair,' Jasmin remarked. 'Olivia doesn't look much like you, Hannah, does she? She's very pretty.'

'Thanks,' I said.

Jasmin looked aghast. 'Oh, sorry, Hannah, I didn't mean—'

'There's the sandpit, Jasmin.' Georgie pointed across the playground. 'Go and dig a big hole and jump into it.'

'Never mind.' I grinned at the look on Jasmin's face. 'Have you seen what they're doing?'

We all stared at Olivia and her mates, eyeing the thin curls of white smoke that drifted around them.

'Well, they *could've* accidentally set themselves on fire and not realised it,' Georgie replied. 'But I'd say they were smoking.'

'Oh!' Jasmin was round-eyed with surprise. 'Is Olivia allowed?'

'Are you joking?' I shrugged. 'My dad's a fitness freak. He'd *kill* Olivia if he knew she was smoking.'

'Great opportunity for blackmail, then,' Lauren remarked, her blue eyes twinkling with glee.

'Hey, I'm not a telltale,' I said quickly. But it *had* given me an idea...

Jasmin suggested that we mooch around the park for a bit, but Katy had to go quite soon after that, so I scooted off too. I was eager to put my plan into action.

When I let myself into the house, Mum and Dad were in the study, talking business, but Dad's mobile was lying on the hall table where he always chucked it when he came in. Perfect.

Quickly I scrolled through the contacts listed in his phone book until I found *Olivia*. Keeping an ear out for Mum and Dad, I tapped Olivia's number into my own phone. Then I slipped upstairs to my bedroom and sent her a text.

You have a secret!

I didn't know if Olivia would recognise my number or not, but it didn't matter if she guessed it was from me. For the moment I had the upper hand and I was *really* curious to find out what Olivia would do...

I didn't have to wait long. I was lying on my bed reading when I heard the front door open and slam at 5.45 pm. Five minutes later footsteps stomped up the stairs and my bedroom door was flung open.

Olivia stood in the doorway and glared at me, one hand aggressively on her hip, the other holding up her phone.

'Oh, like, very funny, Hannah, ha ha ha,' she said, her lip curling. 'Did you think I wouldn't *guess* that this stupid and frankly *childish* text was from you?'

'How do you know?' I asked calmly, turning a page of my book. I was secretly hoping to trap her into admitting that she'd sent me the same text.

'Because I checked Dad's phone to get your number,' Olivia retorted swiftly. 'The same way you got *my* number, I suppose.'

I shrugged. 'It's not nice to get strange texts from people who don't even sign them, is it?' I asked pointedly.

Olivia rolled her eyes. 'Just shut up,' she snapped. 'I've had enough of your weird behaviour. Don't text me again, Hannah. Don't speak to me. Don't look at me. Hell, don't even breathe the same *air* as me, and we'll get on just fine. Understood?' She stabbed viciously at the buttons of her phone as she deleted my text. 'And for your information, I do *not* have a secret.'

I smiled. 'I was at Silver Beech Park this afternoon with my mates.'

Olivia stared at me, a dismayed look creeping across her face. 'So?' she said, trying to sound indifferent.

'Funnily enough, it was quite *smoky* around there,' I added.

'Oh, and you couldn't wait to rush home and spill the beans to Daddy about your delinquent half-sister,' Olivia sneered.

I shook my head. 'I haven't and I won't,' I said. 'Not unless you mess everything up for me.'

Olivia stared at me scornfully. 'You are *seriously* strange, Hannah,' she said. 'Go on, then, tell Dad. I dare you.' She smiled. 'I'll say you made it up to get me into trouble.'

'Olivia!' That was Mum calling from downstairs. 'You're supposed to be cooking dinner.'

Olivia heaved a huge sigh. 'This is worse than living with my own mother,' she muttered, and stomped away.

Frowning, I rolled off the bed and began to pace anxiously up and down my room. I wasn't *exactly* sure who'd got the better of whom in that conversation. Maybe it hadn't been such a good idea of mine to try a bit of blackmail, after all… But now that we were both in the same boat, both keeping secrets from Dad, surely Olivia would leave me alone? Or perhaps she'd be even keener to find out my secret, because then she could maybe use that to deflect Dad's anger when he discovered she'd started smoking?

Things were coming to a crisis point, I realised. One way or another, it was make or break time.

I took a different route to Grandpa's after training the following day. It meant a longer walk from another bus stop, but I was trying to throw Olivia off the scent, just in case she was thinking about secretly following me. Somehow I had to decide exactly how and when I was going to confess everything to Dad. While that was my scariest option by far, it would be better than him hearing it from Olivia. And I needed to do it soon, before Olivia did it first and *really* stuck the knife in.

I was dying to see Grandpa and tell him how well the session had gone this morning. It had been one of those days where everything was right. The sun was shining, the sky was blue and cloudless, and running around on a pitch with a football at my feet just seemed like the best thing in the whole world. Jasmin, Lauren and the others had all been in a great mood too, and we'd laughed and joked our way through the session and then gone for milkshakes and doughnuts afterwards. They'd been really thrilled when I told them that Friday's sleepover was definitely on. I was looking forward to it now. I couldn't wait!

I hung around Grandpa's house for a moment or two, glancing up and down the street in case Olivia appeared. She didn't, so I slipped up the path to the front door and rang the bell. I'd mentioned to Grandpa that I'd be over again, and he said he'd be in. So I was surprised when no one came to the door. I rang again. Still no one.

I frowned. Maybe Grandpa had popped to the shop. But the living-room window was open.

'Mee-yow!'

I got the fright of my life as Sheba suddenly leapt outside onto the window ledge from inside the living room.

'Sheba, you scared me!' I gasped, going over to her.

As I did so, I glanced through the living-room window. Grandpa lay on the floor, very pale and very still.

CHAPTER NINE

'Oh God!' I couldn't believe what I was seeing. '*Grandpa*! Grandpa, are you all right?'

He didn't move. Sheba let out a blood-curdling yowl and jumped back down into the living room again.

What should I do? *What should I do?* My heart was racing, my mind had gone completely blank. I couldn't even tell from here if Grandpa was breathing or not.

Scrambling up onto the ledge, I pushed the window open as wide as it would go. There was just enough of a gap now for me to squeeze through, and

I did so with much straining and panting. Then I jumped down and hurtled over to Grandpa.

Trembling, I knelt down beside him. Dad had insisted that he and I attend a first aid course last year – he'd said that knowing basic first aid was a useful skill for anyone who played sport regularly. But practising on a dummy was different to when someone you cared about was in trouble. Now I couldn't even remember where to start.

I took a deep breath, but it didn't seem to help. I felt sick with panic and knew I had to give myself a good talking-to.

Come on, Hannah. This could be serious. It's up to you. You know what to do. DO IT.

Then, miraculously, my mind cleared.

'Grandpa,' I said loudly, kneeling on the rug beside him. At the same time I was rooting in my pocket for my phone. 'Can you hear me? Can you open your eyes?'

I gently shook Grandpa by the shoulder as I spoke, but he didn't respond in any way. I couldn't see any obvious injuries anywhere. Then, as I bent closer, I could feel his breath on my cheek and see his chest rising and falling slightly. So I knew he was alive. I fought back the tears that welled in my eyes. *No time for that now, Hannah.*

Quickly I checked inside Grandpa's mouth to make sure his airways were clear. Then I turned him over on his side into the recovery position and dialled 999 with shaky fingers while Sheba sat on the arm of the sofa, keeping watch.

'I need an ambulance,' I told the operator when she answered. 'Forty-five, Seymour Terrace. My grandfather's collapsed.'

'Is he conscious?' the operator asked.

I swallowed. 'No, but I've checked and he's breathing and I can't see any sign of injuries. I've put him in the recovery position.'

'Good girl,' the operator said approvingly. 'Now I want you to keep an eye out for the ambulance and take the paramedics straight to your grandfather when they arrive.'

I rang off.

'Please be OK, Grandpa,' I whispered. Then I ran to stand by the window and watch for the ambulance.

It was there in seven minutes, but it seemed like seventy. Sheba went mental when the paramedics invaded her territory and she began to screech loudly, so I had to coax her into the kitchen with a tin of tuna and shut her in there. When I finally went back to the living room, the paramedics had Grandpa on a stretcher.

'We can't say exactly what happened, so we'll have to take him into the hospital for some tests,' one of them said gently. 'You did well, love.'

At that moment Grandpa's eyes fluttered open. Tears of utter relief began to roll silently down my face.

'Hannah,' he mouthed at me.

I took his hand and squeezed it gently.

'Sheba,' Grandpa went on in a feeble voice.

'Don't worry, Grandpa,' I said immediately. 'I'll look after her.'

Grandpa nodded slightly and his eyes closed again.

'Do you want to go with him in the ambulance, love?' the paramedic asked.

I desperately wanted to, but I knew I couldn't. There was something else that had to be done.

'No,' I replied. 'I'd better go home and—' I gulped, 'tell my mum and dad.'

When the ambulance had gone, I found Grandpa's keys so that I could lock up the house. Then I edged my way into the kitchen. Sheba, who had demolished half a tin of tuna and licked the plate clean, was sitting on the worktop glaring at me with pale blue eyes.

'Like it or not, Sheba, I'm all you've got for the moment,' I said with a sigh. 'And believe me, things are going to get a lot worse when we get home...'

It took me half an hour to find Sheba's cat basket and manoeuvre her into it by means of more tuna blackmail. She looked mortally offended and howled piteously all the way home on the bus. People were staring accusingly at me as if I'd tried to murder her or something. But I ignored them. I was trying to work out what I was going to say to Mum and Dad.

I felt like I was going to faint with nerves when I reached our front door. I think my tension had got to Sheba, too, because she'd fallen silent and was crouched in her basket, looking glum. She'd even stopped trying to scratch me through the bars.

I was just about to put my key in the lock when the door was flung open.

'Hannah, where on earth have you been?' Mum cried. 'I was starting to get worried...'

At that moment her gaze fell on the cat basket. Sheba immediately perked up at the sight of this new enemy, and she began to hiss.

'Hannah!' Mum exclaimed, looking totally bewildered. 'What on earth's going on? Why have you got a cat with you?'

'Let me come in and I'll tell you,' I said shakily. 'It's a long story.'

Still looking confused, Mum stood back and held the door open for me. I stepped inside and put Sheba's basket down. At that moment Dad came out of the living room, carrying a newspaper, and I almost turned around and left again. But there was no going back now.

'Hannah, where've you been?' he demanded. 'You know you're supposed to text every couple of hours...' His voice died away as he spotted Sheba for the first time. 'What's that?'

'A cat,' I replied.

'I can see that,' Dad replied impatiently as Olivia stuck her head round the living-room door, a look of rampant curiosity on her face. Oh boy, she was *really* going to enjoy this. 'What I meant was, where's it come from?'

'Her name's Sheba,' I said quietly, 'and she's Grandpa's cat.'

'Grandpa?' Dad was looking thoroughly confused by now. 'Gramps and Nan Phillips don't have a cat.'

This is it, Hannah. But surprisingly, my voice sounded quite calm. 'Grandpa *Fleetwood*'s cat, Dad.'

'Grandpa Fleetwood...' Dad frowned for a second, still looking confused. Then it hit him. His mouth literally fell wide open. 'Grandpa *Fleetwood*?' he spluttered. 'You mean, my *father*?'

I nodded. There was no way back now. 'I've been visiting him since just after Christmas,' I explained in a rush. 'I got his address from the card he sent. But when I went there this afternoon after training finished, he was—'

'*Hannah!*' Dad exploded with fury. But all of a sudden I wasn't scared. Well, not *that* scared, anyway. Because I knew that somehow I was going to carry on seeing Grandpa, and nothing would stop me, not even Dad. 'How dare you do such a thing! You've been going to visit my father all this time, and your mum and I knew nothing about it?'

Mum was staring at me in disbelief. She looked angry, hurt and upset. I felt extremely guilty.

'Hannah, it's just not *like* you to lie and keep things from us!' Mum exclaimed, shaking her head. 'How *could* you? I'm very disappointed in you.'

'I didn't *want* to visit Grandpa in secret!' I burst

out desperately. 'But I *had* to! Dad wouldn't talk about him.'

'And exactly *how many times* have you visited him without my knowledge, Hannah?' Dad demanded, shaking with anger.

'Four,' I mumbled, staring at my feet. 'No, five, including today.'

Dad paced up and down the hall. He seemed unable to say anything as he took all this in.

'So Hannah's got to know Grandpa Fleetwood,' Olivia muttered sulkily. She seemed just as shocked as Mum and Dad, so I'd been right all along. Olivia *hadn't* known what my secret was. 'That's not fair! He's *my* grandfather just as much as Hannah's—'

'Be quiet, Olivia!' Dad ordered. He looked so distressed, I couldn't help feeling sorry for him. 'I would never have *believed* that you'd let me down like this, Hannah.'

'Matt, wait.' Mum spoke very quietly. 'Maybe we should talk about this.'

'*Talk!*' Dad repeated. 'There's nothing to talk about.'

'Yes, there is,' Mum replied. She turned to me, frowning. 'I'm *really* angry and upset that you've deceived us like this, Hannah,' she said. 'I'd never have believed you were capable of it.'

I hung my head, feeling wretched. 'Sorry,' I mumbled.

'You should be,' Mum said sternly. Then she turned to Dad and put her hand on his arm. 'But you know, Matt, maybe it *is* time to start building bridges with Jack.'

Dad stared at Mum as if she was mad. He just wasn't used to her standing up to him.

'What are you saying, Louise? That I should forgive and forget? Because believe me, that's never going to happen.'

At that moment Sheba decided that she'd had enough of not being the centre of attention, and she let out a high-pitched screech.

'Can't you shut that animal up, Hannah?' Dad snapped, clapping his hands over his ears. 'And what's it doing here, anyway?' He scowled at me and at Sheba. 'I suppose this is all Dad's idea?'

I shook my head. 'It was *my* idea to bring Sheba home,' I said defiantly. 'I had no choice. When I got to Grandpa's today, he'd collapsed. I called an ambulance and they took him to hospital—'

'Oh my God!' Mum exclaimed, putting a hand to her mouth.

Dad had suddenly gone quiet. He sagged a little as all the fighting spirit seemed to flood out of him.

'Was he...?' he began in a voice that shook. 'Is he...?'

'He came round just before the ambulance left,' I replied. I was beginning to feel the effects of everything that had happened today and my legs felt as wobbly as jelly underneath me. I sat down on the stairs, keeping Sheba's basket close to me. I wasn't going to let *anyone* take her away, not after I'd promised Grandpa I'd look after her. 'They didn't know what had happened, so they've taken him to hospital for some tests.'

There was silence in the hallway as we all stared at each other. Dad looked greyer and older suddenly, like he'd aged about ten years.

'Matt, I'm going to ring the hospital,' Mum said urgently. 'We have to find out how he is.'

'I want to go and see him,' I said. Now that I was in so much trouble anyway, it didn't matter if I made things worse.

'Me too,' Olivia chimed in. She shot me a stony look. 'I think it's about time I met *my* grandfather.'

Dad stayed silent, head bowed.

I picked up the cat basket as Mum rang the

hospital. I couldn't stay and listen in case it was bad news. Instead I went into the kitchen, closed the door and let Sheba out of her basket. She stepped out elegantly, looking very suspicious as she sniffed the air. Then she began to explore, padding across the floor tiles, tail upright.

Please don't die, Grandpa...

The door opened and Mum came in.

'He's going to be all right, Han,' she said shakily.

I burst into tears of relief. Then I flew across the kitchen and into her arms as Sheba watched us sulkily.

'It wasn't anything serious, honey,' Mum murmured into my hair, holding me close. 'They think his blood sugar was low, and that's why he fainted.'

'I'm sorry for everything I did, Mum,' I bawled like a little kid, 'I'm *really* sorry. But I want to see him. I don't care what Dad says.'

'Ssh.' Mum wiped my face with her fingers like she used to do when I was a toddler. 'Let's feed Sheba and then we'll go.'

I'd brought cat food from Grandpa's house, so I spooned some into a dish. We gave Sheba some milk too and then we left her, grumbling loudly, shut up in the kitchen.

Olivia was standing near the front door with her coat on. There was no sign of Dad.

'I want to come too,' she said, looking pleadingly at Mum.

'Of course, Olivia,' Mum agreed.

The three of us went outside without speaking. As Mum unlocked her car, which was on the drive, Dad appeared at the door. My heart leapt with hope.

'Do you want to drive, Matt?' Mum asked, holding up the keys as Dad came to join us. Dad was a terrible passenger, a real back-seat driver.

Dad shook his head. 'I don't think I could concentrate,' he replied, and that was all he said on the journey to the hospital. In fact, it was all any of us said. Even Olivia was quiet.

Grandpa was in a ward on the second floor of the hospital.

'You go in first and say hello, Hannah,' Mum murmured to me as we stood in the lift. 'Your dad and I will speak to the doctor.'

Grandpa was lying very still, his eyes closed, when I slipped into the ward. But I could see that he had a bit more colour in his face than the last, scary time I'd seen him.

Smiling, I sat down on the chair at the side of the bed and gently touched his hand. Grandpa's eyelids fluttered open.

'Hannah!' He smiled at me. 'What are you doing here?'

'What do you think?' I replied. 'Visiting you, of course. You gave me a bit of a scare.'

'Sorry, love.' Grandpa pulled a face at me. 'I frightened myself too. But I'm going to be just fine.' He smile got broader. 'And you're a real little star, according to the guys who brought me in here. You did all the right things.'

I shrugged. 'Well, Dad and I did this first aid course a little while ago...'

I stopped at the look on Grandpa's face when I mentioned my dad.

'Did you take Sheba home with you, love?' Grandpa asked anxiously. 'You must have got into a whole heap of trouble. I should have thought—'

'It's fine, Grandpa,' I said quickly. 'Sheba's OK, she was on our kitchen worktop trying to open the bread bin when we left.'

'But your dad—?'

'Dad's here,' I said.

A look of hope flared briefly in Grandpa's eyes.

'How is he? Mad at you, *and* at me, I expect.'

'Dad was angry with me for lying to him, but he's *here*,' I explained. 'So are Mum and Olivia. Now you and Dad can sort things out, once and for all.'

Grandpa chuckled. 'You're a chip off the old block, Hannah. I'm so glad I finally met you after all these years.'

'Me too.' I took his hand and held it. 'At least everything's out in the open now.' I didn't dare to think about what might happen next, though.

The door opened and Mum and Olivia came in. Dad was behind them, looking supremely uncomfortable. Mum and Olivia came over to the bed to join me, but Dad remained in the shadows near the door. He looked like he was about to make a run for it at any moment.

'Hello, Jack,' Mum said warmly, smiling at Grandpa. 'I'm Louise. It's lovely to meet you at last.'

'You too, Louise.' Grandpa patted Mum's hand. He looked just as uncomfortable as Dad. 'And you must be Olivia?'

Olivia nodded. 'It's great to see you, Grandpa Fleetwood,' she said. 'But it's a shame Hannah didn't let us know that she was visiting you.' She threw me a sulky glance across the bed.

'I always get left out of *everything*.'

'Olivia!' I said crossly. 'Don't start!' Why did she always have to spoil things? At least now that my secret was out, Olivia didn't have any kind of hold over me any longer.

'Right, girls, we don't want to tire your grandpa out,' Mum said briskly. She hustled Olivia over to the door and beckoned to me. 'Besides, I'm sure your dad wants to have a word.'

Dad still stood there silently. He didn't say a single word.

'Matt?' Mum said hesitantly.

She, Olivia and I stared at Dad. But he wouldn't look at us. He seemed to be fighting some sort of battle with himself. Then, at last, Dad nodded. I let out a huge breath of relief.

Outside the room, Mum, Olivia and I didn't say much. Olivia stood by the window, staring outside, and Mum went to the drinks machine to get some coffee. Meanwhile I flicked through a magazine filled with gossip about celebrities. But I couldn't take any of it in. My own life was a whole lot more interesting to me at the moment than a story in a glossy magazine.

Dad seemed to be gone for a very long time. It

was around twenty minutes before he appeared at the doors again, and I studied him intently. He was pale and his eyes were watery and a bit red, but all the tension seemed to have seeped out of him. He gave both me and Olivia a hug, and then put his arm around Mum.

'Let's go home,' was all he said.

When we were in the car, Dad began to talk. I guess it was easier for him because he was next to Mum, who was driving, and Olivia and I were in the back, so he didn't have to look at us.

'I think you two girls finally deserve an explanation and an apology,' Dad said, staring straight ahead. 'I want you to understand why your grandfather and I fell out all those years ago...'

I was on the edge of my seat, and I could see that Olivia was too.

'When I was a kid, I was the best footballer in my school,' Dad went on quietly. 'Everyone thought I had the talent to turn professional, and your grandfather encouraged me to train hard and get better. I—' Dad stopped, searching for the right words. 'I enjoyed all the praise and attention, but I didn't like the training so much. One of the reasons was that your grandpa was much harder on me than on any of the other players. We argued about it all the time. But why did I need to train so hard? I said to myself. I was a fantastic player, anyway. Showy and flash. I could do loads of tricks with the ball.'

There was another pause.

'Then, when I was around thirteen, your grandfather told me he didn't think I'd make it at a professional level,' Dad muttered so quietly, I could only just hear him. 'I thought he was jealous because *he'd* never had that chance, and I was determined to prove him wrong. For the next few years, I nagged and nagged my dad to use his contacts to get me a trial at a professional club.'

I knew this story back to front, I'd heard it so often. Surprisingly, Dad had turned Chelsea's offer down and opted for university instead.

Dad sighed. 'Eventually my dad gave in. But Chelsea didn't want me, and I couldn't get a trial with anyone else.'

I sat bolt upright in my seat, unable to believe what I was hearing.

'Your grandpa had this "I told you so" attitude that I just couldn't handle,' Dad admitted. 'I asked him to help me find a place at another top club, but he refused. He insisted that I just wouldn't cut it as a professional at the highest level.'

'What happened next?' I asked, hanging on Dad's every word.

'I really believed that my dad had ruined my life. I didn't speak to him again. I left home and moved in with my gran and then I went off to university. I just couldn't forgive your grandfather for being right. I'm sorry, girls.' Dad's voice cracked with emotion a little. 'I know I should have told you all this before. But somehow I just couldn't. I'm truly sorry.'

I was silent, and so was Olivia. I had a strange sensation of my world being turned upside down as things I believed were true suddenly turned out to be false. My family history was being rewritten, and it was a very strange feeling. I knew how difficult it must have been for my dad to tell Olivia and me all this. He never wanted to admit to any weakness. He'd always had this thing about being a strong character, and always being in the right. Except that he wasn't... I thought about all those wasted years when I could have had Grandpa in my life, and a slow, deep anger began to stir inside me.

'Well, that's all behind us now, I hope,' Mum said

quietly. 'Jack's going to be part of our family from now on. Isn't he, Matt?'

There was a nervous edge to Mum's voice. I don't think she was used to seeing this new, vulnerable side of Dad any more than I was.

'Yes, Louise,' Dad agreed at last. 'I think it's time to let go of the past.'

'You won't regret it, darling,' Mum said, sounding very relieved. 'It's the best thing for all of us.'

'Oh good, so now *I'll* finally have a chance to get to know Grandpa Fleetwood!' Olivia said petulantly.

I rolled my eyes. God, it was *so* all about her, wasn't it? But still I couldn't say anything. I was too angry. I felt hugely resentful of the way Dad had put so much pressure on me to be a fantastic footballer. After all, as I'd just discovered, he'd failed at that himself, hadn't he?

Sheba had been having a fine old time in the kitchen while we were gone. She'd knocked over the washing-up liquid, left soapy footprints all over the worktops and peed in the sink. She seemed pleased to see me, though, and actually allowed me to pick her up. I helped Mum clear up and then, absolutely exhausted, I took Sheba and went to my bedroom to watch TV in peace.

'Hannah?' Dad called me from his study as I went past the open door.

'Yes, Dad?' I replied reluctantly. I really didn't want to talk to him right now when I was feeling so furiously churned up inside.

Dad got up from his computer and came over to the door. I put Sheba down and she began clawing viciously at the carpet.

'Talk to me, Hannah.' Dad fixed me with that direct stare of his. I'd always thought a direct stare meant that someone was being honest with you. But Dad had been lying to me for *years*. 'You do believe I'm really sorry for everything, don't you?'

I bit my lip. I could let this go and pretend everything was OK, but why should I? That wasn't how I *felt*.

'You lied to me, Dad!' I burst out. 'You told me over and over again how you could've been a top footballer, and it just wasn't true. But you used that to put more pressure on me! Do you know how much I *hate* you standing on the sidelines shouting at me during every game?'

Dad looked stricken. 'I...didn't know, Hannah,' he mumbled sheepishly. 'I was just trying to help.'

'Well, I get so stressed, it actually makes me play worse, not better,' I retorted. 'And all the other girls think I'm daft to put up with it.'

'I'm sorry, Hannah.' Dad heaved a huge sigh. 'I've always prided myself on being honest and upfront with my kids, as well as approachable, but I've failed miserably, haven't I? Please, love, can we try again?' Dad reached out and put his hand on my shoulder, and I felt some of my anger and bitterness begin to fade.

'Dad, I know you're trying to help me, but like you, I'm never going to be a professional footballer,' I said earnestly, the words tumbling out of me more easily than ever before. 'I love footie, and I'll carry on playing for as long as I want to. I might even do the courses when I'm older, and become a part-time coach like Grandpa was. But Hannah Fleetwood, Captain of the England Women's Football Team – well, that's just not going to happen.'

Dad raked his fingers through his hair, looking very sheepish. 'I've always known that really, Han. I just get a bit carried away at games. Can you forgive me?'

'I want to *enjoy* my football, Dad,' I explained. 'It's a hobby, that's all. I'm sorry if you're disappointed, but that's how it is.'

'Hannah, it's not your fault,' Dad said. 'It's mine. That was just me being all pushy and perfectionist again.'

'Nobody's perfect, Dad.' I managed a faint smile, even though I was still feeling a bit raw and emotional. 'Not even you.'

'Oi, cheeky!' Dad put his arms around me and gave me a squeeze. 'I'm going to try really hard to stop yelling at your matches from now on, Hannah. I promise.'

'In that case,' I said, 'you can start on Saturday morning. The training sessions are closed to spectators, but it turns out the girls who've been on the course are playing an exhibition match, and parents are invited.'

'Is that so?' Dad grinned at me. 'My very first test, then.'

I nodded. I was too exhausted to feel as angry as I'd done earlier, and I could see that Dad was trying very hard to make things up to me. But he wasn't off the hook yet. I wanted to see if he would behave himself on Saturday...

'By the way, your grandfather was saying what a good football player you are,' Dad went on.

'He was?' I beamed, feeling a warm glow inside.

Dad nodded. 'He's very proud of you, and so am I. I'm really glad we had this conversation, Hannah.'

'Me too,' I said, and I meant it. I felt a little more light-hearted as my problems seemed to be sorting themselves out slowly, one by one.

Well, not *all* of them. As we hugged tightly, I caught a glimpse of Olivia watching us from the hallway. I don't know why, but she looked furious. And very upset.

That was her problem, though, not mine. She didn't have a hold over me any more now. I was free.

CHAPTER TEN

'So everything's OK and sorted now with your grandfather and your dad, Hannah?' Grace asked as we ran down the corridor towards the pitch the following morning. 'You've had an enormous smile on your face ever since you arrived for training.'

I'd texted the others yesterday with a very brief description of events, but I was looking forward to telling them the whole story in much more detail later.

'Yep, all sorted,' I said, still smiling, 'My grandpa's coming to visit us today after he comes out of hospital.'

'Cool!' Lauren exclaimed, her eyes as big as saucers. 'Way to go, Hannah!'

'Give us all the details, Han,' Jasmin begged.

'It's a long one,' I replied, 'I'll tell all at the sleepover tonight. And I'm *really* glad that you can come too, Katy.' I grinned at her. 'But the best thing is, we're looking after Grandpa's cat, Sheba, while he's in hospital and she's *really* winding Olivia up. They're both drama queens, but Sheba's miles ahead.'

Olivia had been furious this morning when she found Sheba asleep and shedding cream-coloured hairs on her black D&G jacket. She'd been in a foul mood ever since the day before and our relationship was at an all-time low, but I didn't care. It was all Olivia's fault anyway for sending that horrible, cryptic text to me, so *she'd* started it.

As we left the players' tunnel and headed across the grass to join the other girls, Katy glanced back over her shoulder.

'I wonder where Georgie is?' she remarked. 'She's never late for training.'

'Maybe she missed the bus,' Grace suggested, targeting one of the balls lying on the grass and flipping it up into the air. She headed it to Katy, who trapped the ball neatly on her chest and brought it down. 'I don't think Martha and Mike have noticed she's not here yet, though, so she might just make it without getting an earful from Martha the Misery.'

'Right, let's get started, girls,' Mike yelled.

As we gathered around the two coaches, Georgie pelted full-tilt out of the players' tunnel, her face red.

'Hello you, have a good lie-in?' Lauren said teasingly.

Georgie's face darkened. 'Don't start, Lauren,' she snapped. Then folding her arms, she stood there staring straight ahead of her, not even so much as glancing at us.

'What's all *that* about!' Lauren whispered.

We stared at Georgie, who didn't even so much as glance back at us.

Katy looked anxious. 'Something's wrong.'

'Oh, you *think*?' Lauren retorted in a low voice.

'Stop it,' I whispered. 'This is about Georgie. Let's not start fighting among ourselves.'

For a moment I thought Lauren was going to snap back at me. But then she shrugged and gave me a little smile. 'Since when did *you* get so sensible, Hannah Fleetwood?'

'Oh, I've always been sensible,' I replied, feeling a sudden surge of confidence that I'd spoken up and not just let Grace take charge. 'I hide it well, that's all.'

'So what's going on with Georgie, then?' Jasmin wanted to know.

The five of us were gathered together in a little huddle, whispering, so that Georgie couldn't hear us. Suddenly we realised that no one else, not even the coaches, was talking. We turned round and saw that everyone, including Mike and Martha, were staring at us. No, correction, Mike and Martha were giving us the evil eye.

'*If* we can get on, please,' Mike said firmly. 'Now, after our warm-up we're going to be concentrating on developing skills for dead-ball situations today. Then we're going to finish with a fun six-a-side knock-out tournament.'

It was obvious from early on in the training session that Georgie wasn't going to snap out of her black mood. We had to get into pairs for warm-up activities, and none of us really wanted to partner Georgie. I was secretly glad that Grace asked her first.

'You OK with me, then, Georgie?' Grace said easily, in her usual friendly manner.

Georgie nodded. 'Whatever,' she mumbled, staring down at her feet.

'Ooh, Grace is brave!' Jasmin whispered to me as we passed the ball between us. She and I had paired up, and Lauren was with Katy. 'Georgie's being *totally* off, isn't she? Do you think we've upset her?'

I shrugged. 'I can't think how.'

'Oh, I've just remembered!' Jasmin gasped, chipping the ball to me. 'What about the sleepover tonight, Hannah?'

'God, yes!' My heart plummeted as I glanced over at Georgie's grim expression. 'I hope she's cheered up a bit by the end of training.'

No chance. I was watching Georgie most of the time and she didn't even crack a smile once. In fact, for sheer grumpiness she was giving Martha a run for her money.

'Right, we'll finish off with six-a-side,' Mike said briskly. 'Team one – Grace, Lauren, Jasmin, Katy, Hannah and Georgie. As you all play for the same team, girls, this is a good opportunity to put some of those dead-ball tactics that we practised today into operation. To start off the tournament, you'll play team two, who are...'

As Mike called out the next set of names, Grace nudged me.

'I'm glad Georgie's in goal,' she whispered behind

her long blonde hair. 'At least we can keep out of her way.'

Georgie didn't look at the rest of us as she stomped over to her goalmouth. She stared down at the ground and kicked moodily at a tuft of grass in front of her.

'Oh, I'm really nervous now,' Jasmin confided as we took our places on the pitch alongside the other team. 'I can feel Georgie's eyes *boring* into the back of me!'

'Just ignore her,' Grace advised. 'She's being a real pain in the butt today. There's obviously something wrong, but she's not saying.'

We kicked off, and our opponents immediately took possession.

'Jasmin, tackle Sally!' Georgie yelled furiously from the goal. 'Get on with it, what are you waiting for – a bus? MOVE!'

Looking upset, Jasmin lunged at Sally Burton and missed as Sally nutmegged her neatly and ran on. Katy came across and managed to block Sally's path to goal. But to my amazement, Georgie came charging out, shouldered Katy aside and kicked the ball off Sally's toe as she prepared to shoot.

'What did you do *that* for, Georgie?' Katy cried,

looking angrier than I'd ever seen her. 'I had it covered!'

'No, you didn't,' Georgie snapped. 'God, this team is so useless – I always have to do *everything* myself!'

She threw her eyes up to the heavens and marched back to her goal. We all stared at her in disbelief, even the girls on the other team.

'I'm not enjoying this one bit, Hannah!' Jasmin whispered to me as we kicked off again.

This time a brilliant exchange of passes between Grace and Lauren led them right up to the Deepdale goal. No thanks to Georgie, though, who was yelling at them the whole time.

'Don't be so selfish, Lauren!' Georgie screamed. 'Pass to Grace!' She gave a cry of frustration as Lauren, realising that Grace was being closely marked, took a shot herself and missed the goal by centimetres. 'I knew it! Call that a decent strike? You couldn't strike a match!'

Lauren spun round, her face white with anger.

'Right!' Lauren went storming off down the pitch, Grace, Jasmin and I chasing after her. 'I'm going to tell Georgie *exactly* what I think of her!'

'Leave it, Lauren.' Katy moved across quickly to stop Lauren in her tracks. 'We'll sort it out later.'

Lauren nodded tightly, but I could see she was fuming. Needless to say, we lost 2-0, so we were knocked out of the mini-tournament. We went to sit in the stands to watch the other games, and Georgie sat by herself at the end of the row.

'Glad to see you've taken all our talks about teamwork so seriously, girls,' Martha remarked as she went to referee the second match.

'Maybe one of us should go and talk to her,' Katy said, glancing across at Georgie, who still looked thunderous.

'No, thank you very much,' Lauren replied, 'I'm too fond of my head to risk it being bitten off.'

'I think we should just leave Georgie alone to get over it,' Grace said with a shrug. 'I tried getting her to open up when we were in pairs, but she wouldn't tell me anything.'

'Guys, what about the sleepover at Hannah's tonight?' wailed Jasmin.

We stared at each other in consternation.

'I'm not coming if Georgie does,' Lauren stated firmly. 'I'm not being mean, but it won't be *any* fun if Georgie's being such a moody old witch.'

'That's true,' Grace admitted. 'Maybe we should cancel?'

'Or we could just go ahead anyway and maybe Georgie won't turn up,' suggested Katy.

'But what if she *does* turn up?' Lauren pointed out. 'We'll be right in the poo then.'

'Georgie might be in a better mood by tonight, anyway,' Jasmin said hopefully.

'Or I could tell her right now that she's got to get her act together and chill out a bit if she still wants to come,' I said, feeling slightly sick. *God, I can't believe I just said that.*

'Are you sure, Hannah?' Grace asked, raising her eyebrows.

'Well, it's *my* sleepover, isn't it?' I replied. To be honest, I'd started really looking forward to getting everyone together at my place, and I was surprised to discover how determined I was not to allow Georgie to spoil things. 'I'll do it when we go to change.'

'You're so brave, Hannah!' Jasmin patted me on the arm.

'Any last requests, Han?' asked Lauren.

I managed a smile. 'Ha ha, very funny.'

When the tournament finished, Georgie jumped to her feet and was off down the tunnel like a rocket. We hurried after her. I'd been rehearsing what I was going to say to her for the last half-hour in my head. I was going to be firm but fair...

Georgie, I don't like to have to say this, but unless you start being a bit nicer, I don't really want you to come to my sleepover tonight after all...

My heart was thundering and my stomach felt like water when we reached the changing-room door.

'Good luck, Hannah,' Katy whispered in my ear.

Georgie was sitting on the bench, pulling off her football boots. She had her head bent so her wild black hair covered her face. I marched over there and stood in front of her.

'Georgie, I don't like to have to say this, but unless...'

Georgie glanced up at me. There were tears in her eyes.

'Georgie!' I exclaimed, horrified. I sank down onto the wooden bench beside her. 'What's up? Why are you crying?'

The others, who had all been keeping a close eye on us from the other side of the changing-room, now rushed over.

'I'm not crying,' Georgie mumbled, ducking her head again. 'S-sorry I was so grumpy today.'

'Oh, never mind that.' Lauren sat down on the

other side of Georgie and put her arm round her. 'Just tell us what's wrong.'

Silently Georgie opened her sports bag and pulled out her Spurs shirt. It had been white once, but now it was pale pink.

'It got put in the wrong load of washing by one of my stupid brothers,' Georgie explained with a sigh. 'I *know* I'm being stupid, but it took me *ages* to save up my pocket money to buy it. Now it's ruined...' Her lips quivered again.

'So that's why you were in such a bad mood,' Katy said softly. 'Why didn't you tell us?'

'Yeah, why didn't you?' Lauren echoed. 'It would have done you good to rant and rave *to* us, rather than *at* us!'

Georgie shrugged. 'I don't like to bother people with my problems,' she muttered sheepishly.

'Well, that'd be a whole lot better than making *us* miserable too,' Grace pointed out. 'Look, Georgie, my mum's got some kind of stuff she bought at the supermarket that goes in the washing machine. It'll take the pink colour out.'

'Really?' Georgie glanced at Grace, her face lighting up with hope. 'Do you think it'll work?'

Grace shrugged. 'It worked when Gemma shoved

her brand-new blue jeans in with a whites wash,' she said. 'Come over to mine, and we'll give it a try.'

'Thanks, Grace.' Georgie jumped up and gave her a big hug. It was quite touching, really, because Georgie's not a huggy type of person at all. 'Sorry again, you lot.'

'So we're mates again now,' Jasmin crowed happily. 'And now we can look forward to Hannah's sleepover, after all. It's going to be *awesome*.'

'I hope so,' I replied, feeling a bit nervous again.

I just hoped that it was awesome in a *good* way...

'Lovely house,' Grandpa said, looking around him as I led him into the living room. He picked up Sheba, who'd run to meet him, purring loudly, and turned to smile at my dad. 'You've done well for yourself, son.'

'Thanks, Dad.'

It was strange to see my dad and *his* dad together. We'd picked Grandpa up from the hospital and brought him to our house for lunch, and at first the conversation in the car had been a bit strained. But Dad and Grandpa were getting to know each other again after a very long time, so it wasn't surprising, really.

'Olivia should be back from her mum's quite soon,' Dad said, sitting down on the sofa next to Grandpa. 'I've been given strict instructions to keep you here until she gets back.'

'Right, time for lunch,' said Mum. 'I'm going to make sure you get a decent meal inside you, Jack. The hospital said they didn't think you'd been eating properly and that was one reason why you collapsed.'

Grandpa looked a bit shamefaced. 'Well, you know how it is, Louise,' he murmured. 'It doesn't seem worth cooking, seeing as I'm on my own.'

'Well, you're not on your own now, Grandpa,' I chimed in. 'I'm going to be visiting you all the time – you won't be able to get rid of me. And after one of Mum's meals, you won't need to eat again for a week, believe me.'

'You mind your manners, Missy,' Mum said mock-sternly as she went to the kitchen.

'Grandpa, will you come and watch my match tomorrow?' I asked eagerly. It was hard to believe how quickly things had changed. A few days ago I was forced to keep my relationship with Grandpa a secret – now here he was, coming to lunch and hopefully to watch me play, all with my parents' approval. 'Maybe we could pick you up on the way there.'

'I'd love to, Hannah,' Grandpa replied, stroking Sheba.

'You know, Dad, you could always stay with us this weekend, if you liked,' my dad offered hesitantly. 'I could take you home on Sunday night.'

Grandpa smiled and shook his head. 'Not yet, Matt, it's early days, and to be honest I'm looking forward to sleeping in my own bed again. But I'd love to come and stay sometime very soon. Anyway, it's Hannah's sleepover tonight, isn't it? I don't want to be in the way!'

'Oh, yes, the sleepover,' I said with a little frown. It would either go brilliantly, or it would end in complete disaster, I thought. There didn't seem to be anything in between when the six of us got together!

I could only wait and see.

CHAPTER ELEVEN

'Come on, Jasmin!' Lauren screamed, 'I can score! I can score! You've just got to run with me!'

'I'm trying!' Jasmin groaned, doubled over with laughter. 'Except I can't move my feet without falling over!'

You might have thought we'd have had enough of football by now. Well, we hadn't. Except that this was football with a difference. Lauren had suggested that we try some different ways of playing the game. First we'd had a rule that the ball couldn't touch the ground; we had to keep it up in the air. Then we'd tried playing *backwards*. Now it was three-legged football. Lauren and Jasmin had their ankles tied together, I was tied to Georgie and Grace was attached to Katy. We were hobbling around the lawn in my back garden, arms around our partners, trying to kick the ball, but we were totally helpless with giggles. My sides hurt so much, I was actually in pain. Lauren's idea had certainly got my sleepover off to a cracking start, though.

'Jasmin, just follow me!' Lauren yelled, straining towards the ball, which was right in front of her and Jasmin. 'Right! Your *left* foot, my *right* foot – now, kick!'

Looking confused, Jasmin struck out with the wrong foot. She toppled over, taking Lauren with her. They both lay there on the grass, screaming with laughter.

'This is our chance, Hannah!' Georgie shouted. 'Let's get that ball! Quick-march! One – two, one – two!'

I missed a beat and stumbled, bringing Georgie down. Meanwhile, Grace and Katy passed by us confidently, legs moving in rhythm, heading for the ball.

'You just need a bit of coordination,' Grace called smugly over her shoulder as she and Katy kicked the ball towards the 'goal', which was between two garden chairs. Unfortunately, though, the ball landed with a splash in the goldfish pond, and Katy rushed to fish it out, forgetting that she was still attached to Grace.

'Help!' Grace shrieked, giggling so much she got hiccups as she was dragged across the lawn.

'This is *so* funny,' I sighed, trying to catch my breath.

'Maybe we should play three-legged at the match tomorrow,' Lauren suggested mischievously. 'I bet Martha would approve.'

'Oh, bum, it's starting to rain.' Jasmin glanced up at the darkening sky. 'I suppose we'd better go in.'

'Yes – hic – let's,' Grace agreed.

'Dad'll be coming to take the pizza orders soon,' I said, leading them into the living room. 'We can watch a DVD while we're stuffing ourselves silly!'

'Excellent idea, Hannah Montana!' Jasmin agreed, rushing over to one of our two sofas and bagging the best viewing position. 'This here seat is mine, officially.'

Georgie, Grace and Katy rushed to join her, arguing good-naturedly over who was going to sit where. Georgie grabbed the second-best TV seat, next to Jasmin, while Grace and Katy sat on the other sofa. Meanwhile, Lauren put the TV on and began flicking through the channels.

'Jasmin, is that your phone?' Grace said, winking at me and the others. They'd dumped their sleepover bags in a corner of the living room, and there was the sound of muffled, tinny music coming from one of them.

'No,' Jasmin retorted. 'So don't try and trick me into getting up, so you can nick my seat!'

Georgie groaned loudly. 'It's mine. Promise you won't pinch my place, Katy?'

'I promise,' Katy replied, an innocent look in her large brown eyes. But as Georgie dived across the room towards her bag, Katy moved smoothly from the other sofa into her vacant spot.

'Sorry, Georgie,' Katy said, smiling, 'I lied!'

Georgie looked so taken aback, we all howled. After a moment, Georgie smiled too. She found her phone, stabbed at the buttons and then gave a loud groan.

'Is something wrong?' I asked.

'Nah, it's just something stupid.' Georgie chucked her phone back in her bag, went across the room and sat down on top of Katy. Katy gave a squeal of protest.

'Sorry, Katy, didn't see you there in *my* seat!' Georgie said, snorting with laughter. Giggling helplessly, Katy moved aside and went back to sit with Grace.

'What films have you got, then, Han?' Lauren asked, peering at the glass shelves full of DVDs. She picked up the one closest to her and gave a great burst of laughter. 'What's *this*?'

'What's what?' I asked.

Lauren held up a very familiar-looking DVD, and my heart couldn't have sunk any further.

'*Hannah Fleetwood, Future Captain of the England Women's Football Team*!' Lauren read out in a deep, gravelly voice like a Hollywood film trailer. '*A story of one young girl's struggle to reach the top in the cut-throat world of professional football. You'll laugh, you'll cry, you'll fall asleep, actually—*'

'It does *not* say all that, Lauren, you big fat liar!' I muttered, hot with embarrassment as I hurtled across the room towards her. But Lauren was already slotting the DVD into the machine.

'What is it, Hannah?' Katy asked curiously.

'Oh, just something my parents put together,' I mumbled, trying to grab the remote control from Lauren. But she wasn't letting go. I'd meant to hide the DVD or throw it away or something, but I'd forgotten. However, I was *sure* it hadn't been lying in full view like that. Someone must have put it there. And I bet I knew *who*.

I was hoping that Lauren wouldn't know how to get our DVD player to work, but by luck or skill, she got it going somehow. The picture kicked in right where I'd cut it off on my birthday, and another clip of our match against Seventrees appeared on the screen. This time the striker I'd fouled in the previous clip turned me neatly, shielding me from the ball with her body, and raced off.

'Hannah!' Dad roared from the sidelines, 'You let her get the wrong side of you! I've told you about this before! Why don't you ever listen?'

Everyone in the room burst out laughing, except me. They all watched wide-eyed as yet another of my mistakes, this time from our last match before the course began, flashed up.

'You mean your mum and dad have made a film of *all* your bad bits, Hannah?' Jasmin giggled. 'That's so mental!'

'Haven't they put any of your good stuff in?' asked Georgie, laughing as Dad started yelling as I lost the ball once more. 'I'd kill my dad if he did this.'

'Lauren, stop it now,' said Katy, glancing at my face.

'Yes, Lauren,' Grace chimed in. 'Turn it off.'

Lauren turned to look at me as I stood next to her, and bit her lip. 'Sorry, Hannah,' she said guiltily, stopping the DVD. 'Didn't mean to upset you. But we were laughing at your dad, not you.'

'Oh, absolutely!' Jasmin exclaimed, and I began to feel a bit better. 'He's just so funny! Sorry, Hannah.'

Georgie nodded. 'Me too. But you have to admit your dad's well over the top, Han.'

'He *was*, but he says he's going to stop,' I reminded them. 'Well, he's going to try, at least.'

'We'll make sure he does, Hannah,' Grace said with a wink. 'There's six of us to keep an eye on him now!'

I grinned. It was *so* cool to have five new friends, all at once!

'OK, what else have we got here, then?' Lauren began sorting through the pile of films. 'Shall we vote on it?'

'Good idea,' I agreed, as Dad came in.

'Pizza time, girls.' Dad waved a bunch of menus at us. 'I'm your waiter for tonight, so let's have the orders.'

We fell on the menus like ravenous beasts.

'Don't let Jasmin decide on the toppings,' Grace said, 'we'll be here all night.'

'Ooh, *so-o-o* unfair!' Jasmin said indignantly. 'I always have my favourite, ham and extra cheese. But I like tuna and onion too...'

We'd just decided what to have when Olivia strolled into the room.

'Oh, hi,' she said coolly. 'Having a good time?'

'Yes, thanks,' I said, eyeballing her. 'We've been choosing a DVD to watch.'

Olivia smirked. I *knew* it was her!

'Do you want pizza, love?' Dad asked her on his way out to the phone.

'No, I'll have a salad,' Olivia replied in a superior manner. 'It's much healthier.'

'Yeah, there are *so* many things that are bad for you, aren't there?' Georgie was in there like a flash. 'Smoking, for instance.'

Olivia's face was a picture. She turned abruptly and went out while we all chuckled quietly.

'I think she'll leave us alone now,' I said cheerfully. 'I'm going to scoot off and get some drinks. You lot choose a DVD – anything that doesn't have *me* in it!'

Humming to myself, I went to the kitchen. Mum was out, but she'd done a supermarket run and bought loads of fizzy drinks and snacky stuff.

I was just getting the glasses out when Olivia slunk in.

'Couldn't wait to blab to your friends, could you?' she muttered.

'Huh?'

'About me *smoking*,' she hissed, giving me the evil eye through her fake eyelashes.

I looked amused. 'Oh, get over yourself, Olivia. I didn't have to say anything. They were with me in the park. They saw you.'

'Just shut up, Hannah.' Olivia's glossed lips curled as she glared at me. 'You think you're so great, don't you? Getting to know Grandpa Fleetwood behind Dad's back. I knew he'd forgive you though, you always *were* Daddy's little girl—'

'I don't know why you're having a go at me,' I broke in, quite coolly. Since my conversation with Dad, I felt a lot stronger, and more able to stand up to Olivia than ever before. She didn't have a hold over me any longer, especially now that my secret wasn't a secret any more. '*You're* the one who gets everything you want. You wanted to move in with us, didn't you? So you ran away to make sure Dad sat up and took notice, and he *did*.'

'I had to.' Olivia's voice wobbled suddenly, which took me completely by surprise. 'He wouldn't have been interested in me otherwise.'

I stared at her. 'Are you crazy?' I demanded. 'You've always been his favourite, he lets you get away with murder.'

'Only because he's not that bothered *what* I do!' Olivia retorted fiercely. Oh God, were those tears in her eyes I could see? 'He doesn't care about me like he cares about you.'

'But Dad's always on my case!' I exclaimed.

'That's because he loves you more,' Olivia said bitterly.

'Oh, that's rubbish.'

'Is it?' Olivia demanded. 'I don't think so. He and Mum split up when I was a baby. I've *never* lived with Dad, not like you. He's been here with you all your life.'

I remembered what Mum had said about Olivia

not really having things her own way all the time, and I suddenly felt a bit ashamed.

'So *that's* why you've been so mean to me all these years?' I said slowly. 'Because you're jealous? That's why you were always putting me down, even when I was *trying* to be nice to you? Why you tried to frighten me with that horrible text?'

Olivia looked puzzled. 'What text?'

'Oh, you know very well!' I snapped. 'All it did was make things between us a lot worse.'

'I didn't send you any text, you idiot!' Olivia yelled. '*You* sent *me* one, remember?'

We stood there in silence as I stared at Olivia uncertainly. She sounded righteously indignant, but then she *was* a good actress. And who else could have sent the text, anyway?

I don't know what would have happened next, but right then Lauren bounced in.

'Oo-er!' she said, looking from me to Olivia. 'Am I interrupting something? I came to help you, Hannah.'

'No, don't worry,' I said. Meanwhile Olivia had turned and gone without another word.

I tried to make sense of what Olivia had said as Lauren and I put glasses on a tray. This was another twist in our family history, and yet I had been so sure that I knew the way things were. But Olivia obviously saw the same situation completely differently. Which of us was right? Maybe neither of us was...

We had our pizzas and watched a comedy film, and then we played *The Legend of Zelda* on Lauren's Wii that she'd brought with her. Sure we had fun, but by the time Dad sent us off to bed, I could sense that things had gone a bit flat. I knew it was mostly my fault for brooding all evening about what Olivia had said.

The six of us were sleeping in my bedroom, which was a bit of a squeeze even though it was a large room. I had my own bed and another single bed as well as two folding camp beds and two blow-up mattresses that took up almost the whole of the available floor space. Lauren and Georgie had already started arguing downstairs about who was having the other bed, and Dad had had to step in and toss a coin for it. Lauren won, much to Georgie's disgust.

'God, Hannah, this is a bit of a weird colour!' Jasmin remarked tactlessly, staring around at the aqua-coloured walls as I led them in. 'I'd feel seasick if I woke up to that every morning.'

'I *like* it,' I said. I was a bit sharp, but that was because I was still raw from my conversation with Olivia.

'Oh, I didn't mean...' Jasmin looked embarrassed. 'No, it's nice, it's just that it might look better without all those football posters on the walls.'

'It's *my* room, Jasmin,' I muttered in a sulky voice. 'I'll do what I want.'

'Time to get changed, everyone,' Grace said firmly.

Trying not to get in each other's way, we all changed into our jim-jams.

'God, Lauren, how old are you?' Georgie remarked, raising her eyebrows as she took in Lauren's candy-pink pyjamas printed with fluffy grey kittens. 'Five?'

Lauren poked her tongue out as she bounced up and down on her bed. 'Sore loser, huh, Georgie?' she asked smugly. 'OK, girls, feast time!'

As we started pooling our chocolate and sweets, I noticed that Katy was looking a bit uncomfortable. She was wearing a very old grey T-shirt for a night-dress that looked as if it had been washed a few hundred times and had a few holes here and there. Katy seemed very embarrassed, even though no one had mentioned it.

'Here, have some Galaxy, Katy.' Lauren held out a large chunk of chocolate.

Katy shook her head. 'I haven't got any to share,' she said quietly.

'Oh, I don't care,' Lauren said with a shrug. 'Have it, anyway. If I eat it all, I'll be sick.'

'No, thank you,' Katy said stubbornly.

'Look, it's only a bit of chocolate I'm offering you, not the Crown Jewels,' Lauren began in an irritated voice.

'We'll have to clean our teeth after this,' Grace said quickly, as Katy frowned at Lauren and shook her head again more firmly.

'Ooh, goodie-goodie Grace strikes again!' Jasmin giggled, chomping on her Snickers bar. Grace glared at her.

'By the way, Dad said we had to turn our phones off now, remember?' I said, trying to change the subject. There was a definite tension in the air that hadn't been there earlier. It was partly my fault, I knew. I was feeling out of sorts after what had happened with Olivia.

There was silence as we all rooted for our phones. Suddenly Grace gave a little shriek as she found hers.

'*Lauren!* Is this from you?'

'What?' Lauren asked, peeping out from underneath the big duvet and looking as innocent as a baby.

'This stupid text!' Grace held up her phone. '*You have a secret admirer! I love you! I kiss your hand!*' she read out.

Lauren burst out laughing. 'How did you know it was me?'

'You forgot to withhold your number this time!' Grace rolled her eyes, looking annoyed. 'You're so *childish*, Lauren. I suppose it was you who sent the other silly text I got yesterday. The one that was supposed to be from a *boy*.'

'Oh, I got a daft text as well,' Jasmin chimed in. 'It said I'd won a million pounds in the lottery.'

'Yeah, I got that one earlier tonight,' Georgie added. 'Like I *believed* it.'

'Me neither,' Jasmin said quickly. 'Well, only for a minute.'

I couldn't say anything. I had just gone ice-cold all over. Had Lauren sent me that mystery text, and not Olivia? No, she couldn't have, I told myself immediately. I was *sure* it was Olivia.

Katy shrugged. 'I had a strange text too. I just assumed it was someone being stupid.' She glanced at Lauren. 'I was right.'

'Oh, lighten up, you boring old grumps,' Lauren muttered sullenly. 'It was just a *joke*.'

I frowned. I'd been saving the full account of my secret and Grandpa Fleetwood and the text from Olivia to tell them now. But maybe there was another twist to this story...

'You didn't send *me* one, did you, Lauren?' I demanded.

'*You have a secret,*' Lauren said with a grin.

I stared at her in mounting horror.

'You didn't know it was me, did you?' Lauren went on, looking very pleased with herself. 'Fooled you!'

I jumped out of bed and almost trampled all over Katy and Grace, who were on the blow-up mattresses next to me. I didn't remember *ever* being so furious in my whole life before.

'Lauren, you *idiot!*' I shouted. Lauren turned pale, looking very taken aback. 'I *did* have a secret, didn't I? I'd started visiting Grandpa Fleetwood and my mum and dad didn't know! I thought that text was from *Olivia* and she was trying to mess with my head or blackmail me or something. I was trying *so* hard to get along with her before then and that text messed everything up, and it upset me so much, I can't tell you!'

'Well, it's not my fault, is it?' Lauren pouted at me. '*I* didn't know you were going to blame Olivia.'

'Shut up and leave me alone!' I hissed. Shaking with rage, I dived back into bed and pulled the duvet over my head.

'Now look what you've done, Lauren,' I heard Katy say.

'Oh, why don't *you* shut up, Katy?' Lauren retorted. 'You think you're so high and mighty—'

'Stop it, Lauren.' That was Grace.

'I don't have to do what *you* say, Grace Kennedy!'

'See what you've done now, Lauren?' Georgie began. 'You've started a big argument.'

'Oh, leave Lauren alone, Georgie!' Jasmin scolded, 'It *was* just a joke.'

I burrowed further under the duvet as an angry silence descended on the room. *Great, just great*, I thought miserably. This surely had to be the most disastrous sleepover since time began.

CHAPTER TWELVE

I didn't sleep very well – surprise – and I woke up quite early. The others were still asleep, and Georgie was snoring.

As I slipped out of bed and into my dressing gown, I glanced over at Lauren. I could just see her ruffled blonde head sticking out from under the duvet.

Maybe I'd been a bit mean to her, I thought ruefully as I went out, careful not to step on anyone along the way. But it had been a *really* stupid and childish thing to do to send that text. Maybe Olivia and I wouldn't have fallen out *quite* so bitterly without that…

I went downstairs to the kitchen. Olivia was in there in her dressing gown, making a cup of coffee.

I took a deep breath. I didn't want to do this, but I knew I had to. 'Sorry,' I said quickly, 'That text I mentioned, the one that upset me – I just found out that it wasn't from you. Sorry.'

Olivia shrugged. 'Whatever,' she replied. But for once, her tone was quite reasonable, and not aggressive.

As Olivia went out, carrying her mug, Dad wandered in.

''Morning, Hannah.' He went over to the coffee machine. 'I think I'd better apologise to you in advance. Just in case I forget myself and shout things at the match today.' He grinned at me. 'Maybe I'd better get your mum to bring along some sticky tape?'

Dad mimed putting sticky tape over his mouth and I managed a faint smile.

'Well, you look full of the joys of spring, Hannie.' Dad stared closely at me. 'Not.'

I sighed. 'Oh, Dad, it's *awful*. We had a big fight last night and now I don't think anyone's going to be speaking to each other this morning.'

There was no point in going into details and

blaming anyone. We'd all been as bad as each other – no, I'd been the *worst*. And at my own sleepover. It was mortifying. And it had been arranged with the other parents that Mum and Dad would take us all straight to the ground for the match, so we were going to have to spend the next few hours together.

Dad chuckled and then quickly tried to turn it into a cough.

'You girls,' he said, shaking his head. 'You seem to be having dramas all the time.'

'When we get on, we get on brilliantly,' I muttered, 'But when it goes wrong – it *really* goes wrong! And I don't know how to make it right again.'

Dad looked thoughtful.

'What about a bonding exercise?' he suggested.

I looked blank.

'Mum and I do them every so often with the people who work for us,' Dad explained. 'Everyone goes on a team-building exercise like mountain-climbing or sailing or paint-balling. You get to know each other better by having fun together, and then that carries over into the workplace.'

'It sounds good,' I said. 'But we don't have much time. It's only a few hours to the match.' I pulled a face. 'And I don't think anything like paint-balling would be a good idea. It could get pretty vicious!'

'Well, I think your mum's planning one of her sumptuous breakfasts,' Dad began, with a twinkle in his eyes.

'She would be,' I groaned.

'Scrambled eggs, freshly squeezed juice, fresh fruit milkshakes, waffles...' Dad raised his eyebrows at me. 'So why don't the six of you make breakfast instead?'

I frowned. 'You think?'

'Anything that gets you working together and relying on each other is a good thing,' Dad said with a grin. 'Trust me, Han.'

I shrugged. Dad hadn't really convinced me but I didn't have any other ideas.

Mum wasn't quite so keen, though, when I asked her permission. She actually looked *nervous* when I suggested that she let us loose with all her shiny chrome gadgets. But I managed to persuade her by promising faithfully to clear up *any* mess straight away.

When I went back to my bedroom, the others were already up. They were all dressing in a cold and frosty silence you would have needed an ice pick to chip your way through.

'Right,' I said breezily. 'Breakfast! And we're making it.'

'I don't want any—' Lauren began sulkily.

'Scrambled eggs, toast, fruity milkshakes, fresh orange juice and waffles,' I went on, ignoring her.

Jasmin actually heaved. 'I only ever have Coco Pops,' she said, looking a bit ill.

'Then today will be a real treat, won't it?' I replied, hustling them all briskly downstairs.

Mum and Dad had laid out everything in the kitchen – eggs and fruit and bread and all the utensils we'd need. Mum had even written down her special recipes for waffle batter and strawberry and vanilla milkshake. Then they'd disappeared into the living room, although Dad had pretty much had to drag Mum away.

'O-*kay*!' I said brightly, wishing this was over. 'Lauren, you can help me make the scrambled eggs. You whisk up the eggs and I'll sort the pan out. Grace and Georgie, you're in charge of the juice machine and the waffle-maker. Jasmin and Katy, you two sit at the table and cut up the strawberries for the milkshakes.'

'I didn't know you were *this* bossy, Hannah,' Lauren muttered as I opened the pack of butter.

I ignored her, and there was silence for the next few minutes. I glanced across at Grace and Georgie. Grace was studying Mum's batter recipe while Georgie glumly sliced oranges. Meanwhile Katy and Jasmin were cutting up the strawberries, but still no one said anything. I sighed as I chucked a lump of butter into the frying pan and switched the gas on. This wasn't working.

'Oops!' Lauren gave a gasp as she clumsily tried to crack an egg into a bowl. She missed completely, and the yolk slid down the side of the bowl and off the edge of the worktop. Quick as a flash, I grabbed the bowl and managed to catch the egg before it hit the floor. Lauren glanced at me and we both began to smile.

'We're a good team, Hannah,' she said, 'You might *just* have noticed that cooking's not my thing at all! Sorry.'

'No, *I'm* the one who should be saying sorry – for everything that happened last night,' I replied, taking my courage in both hands. 'You shouldn't have sent that text, Lauren, but it's not *your* fault that it messed everything up. Things were all wrong, anyway. I've been jealous of Olivia all these years, and then I found out yesterday that *she's* always been jealous of *me*.' I swallowed as I started feeling a bit emotional. 'Anyway, I hope things between me and Olivia are going to be different from now on. But I went a bit over-the-top at you, Lauren, and I'm *really* sorry.'

'Forget it,' Lauren said generously, patting my arm. 'Now help me with these flipping eggs or we'll be here all day! I've got no idea what I'm doing!'

'Ooh, you made up!' Jasmin sighed happily, helping Katy tip the strawberries into the blender. 'I've been *dying* to say that I'm sorry, too. I've got *such* a big mouth and I always say the wrong thing and I can't keep my nose out of anyone else's business—'

'Well, neither can I,' Grace broke in as she whisked up the waffle batter. 'You're not on your own there, Jasmin.'

'And me.' Georgie put down her knife, looking a bit sheepish. 'I'm always saying stuff I wished I hadn't. I've got a bigger mouth than you, Jasmin.'

'Oh no, Georgie, that's not true!' Jasmin exclaimed. She frowned. 'Well, it *is* true, actually.' Then she began to blush. 'See, there I go again! Sorry, Georgie.'

We all grinned.

'Don't ever change, Jasmin,' I said, 'we love you just the way you are!'

Katy had been quiet up till now. She added some milk to the fruit in the blender and replaced the top before turning to look at us.

'I know I can be a pain in the backside,' she said, looking very uncomfortable. 'I don't mean to be so awkward. Sorry.'

Katy was usually so reserved, I knew it must have taken a lot for her to admit this. I went over and slung my arm around her shoulders.

'Group hug!' Lauren shouted, and we all huddled round and almost squeezed the breath out of each other.

'We're all as bad as each other in one way or another,' I said as we broke apart. 'But things are going to be different from now on, right?'

'Well, we can try,' Grace agreed.

'You mean we're not going to argue any more?' Jasmin looked doubtful. 'I think all friends argue *sometimes*.'

'Especially when they're as wild and wacky and wonderful as we are,' Lauren said, her baby-blue eyes twinkling. 'Oh!' She gave a gasp. 'I have an idea! How about we have a special word that we say when someone starts to get all antsy and annoyed, and we think they should calm down a bit?'

'What, to make them stop and think, you mean?' I asked, rushing over to stop the butter from burning in the pan. 'Great idea!'

'Yeah, we'll be like a gang with a special password,' Jasmin said enthusiastically.

'OK, suggestions?' Lauren looked round at us.

'Knickers,' Georgie said.

'Same to you,' Lauren retorted.

'No, I meant, that's my suggestion,' Georgie explained.

Lauren shook her head. 'It needs to be something that's all about *us*.'

'How about *footie*?' said Grace.

'*Footie* is good,' Jasmin agreed, switching on the blender.

'Jasmin, NO!' Katy shrieked.

Everything happened so fast! The second the blender burst into action with a loud whizzing noise, the top flew right off. We all screamed in utter shock as the vanilla-scented mixture of strawberries and milk exploded upwards and outwards like a mini-milkshake volcano. It went *everywhere*. It splashed the worktops, the walls, the floors and everything else in the kitchen. Including us.

'Jasmin, I was *going* to say I wasn't sure I'd put the lid on properly!' Katy groaned, grabbing a whole heap of kitchen roll and trying to clean herself off.

I had milkshake all over my face and in my hair. Wiping my eyes, I glanced at the others. They were soaked too.

'Help!' Jasmin shrieked, shaking herself like a dog and sending droplets spraying everywhere. She'd got the worst of it because she was closest, and her dark hair was covered in pink goo. Meanwhile, Lauren and Georgie and Grace were staring down at their wet, stained clothes in appalled silence.

'Jasmin, you have strawberries stuck in your hair,' I gasped.

Then I began to laugh; I couldn't help it. Georgie was the first to join in, but the others swiftly followed. We were laughing so much, we couldn't even stop when Mum and Dad rushed in, their faces pictures of sheer horror.

'I think I've found the perfect word, guys,' I announced. '*Milkshake*!'

'Look, it's Freya!' Lauren yelled as we reached the football ground.

After breakfast we'd piled into Mum's and Dad's cars and they'd driven us to the ground. Then Dad had gone again, to collect Grandpa Fleetwood. We were all surprised to see our tall blonde coach Freya Reynolds standing on the steps waving at us as we arrived in the car park.

'Hi, Freya,' I said, as we rushed over to her, Mum following behind us. 'We didn't know you were coming to watch today.'

Freya winked at me.

'Well, I like to keep you on your toes! Great to see you, girls. You look like you've had a good week?'

'Oh, we did!' Georgie assured her. 'We've got to know each other better—'

'We've had a fantastic laugh together,' Jasmin chipped in.

'And a few arguments,' Grace added.

'Oh, and we've learned *loads*,' Lauren added. 'Move over, David Beckham. The curl on my free kick is to *die* for.'

'It's been fun,' Katy said with a big grin.

'Well, I can't wait to see you playing together today,' Freya replied eagerly. 'Now, remember what I always say to you on the morning of a match?'

'*Did you have a good breakfast?*' we all said

together, and then we collapsed into fits of giggles. Freya looked surprised.

'What's so funny?' she asked. 'You know how important it is for energy out there on the pitch.'

'Don't worry, Freya, they had a proper breakfast.' Mum raised her eyebrows at us. 'Eventually.' After we'd cleaned up the kitchen, she meant. 'I'll tell you all about it while we're waiting for the match to begin.'

Mum and Freya went off to join the other spectators in the stands while we scooted off to the changing-rooms. There was a lot of joking and fooling around as we got changed because we were all in such a great mood. I was really pleased that Martha and Mike had decided to put the six of us in the same team today, along with the Franklin twins and Sally from Deepdale, and Vicky and Preeti from Shawcross Under-Thirteenss. It would be fan-brill-tastic, according to Lauren, to play a proper match after a week of training. Our team was called – ahem – Martha's Merry Men, and the others were Mike's Musketeers.

There were more people in the stands than we were expecting when we ran out on to the pitch to applause. I spotted Georgie's dad – it wasn't hard, he was as tall as she was! Lauren's glamorous mum was there too, the first time I'd ever seen her at a match. And I recognised Grace's dad; I'd seen him several times before, and he had the exact same-coloured fair hair as Grace. But I couldn't see my own family. Then, as we took our positions for the kick-off, I saw them a few rows back. Mum, Dad, Grandpa Fleetwood and – oh my God! *Olivia!* What on earth was *she* doing here?

'Are you all right, Hannah?' Katy whispered to me as I hurried past her to my place. 'Are you worried about your dad?'

I shook my head. 'We had another chat before we left this morning, and he's already apologised in advance in case he can't stop himself yelling! But no, I'm not worried.' And I wasn't. I *was* wondering what Olivia was doing there, though.

We kicked off and almost immediately it became obvious that our team had the advantage in midfield with Jasmin, Lauren and I getting the biggest share of the ball. Twice in the first ten minutes we sent Grace clear through the opposing defence and she nearly scored both times.

I also quickly realised that because the six of us had got to know each other so much better, this had spilled over into our game and improved it. Several times I knew almost without looking where Jasmin, Lauren and Grace would be when we were going forward, and I could probably have passed fairly accurately to them with my eyes closed.

'This is just fab!' Jasmin murmured to me as we waited for Katy to take a throw-in. 'I kind of *know* what you guys are thinking almost before you do it. It's like we *really* are a team now!'

I hadn't heard my dad shouting at me so far, which was a bonus, but then the stadium was a lot bigger than the pitch we usually played on at the local college. But as Katy threw the ball to Sally Burton, who side-footed it to me, I suddenly heard that familiar voice.

'Look up and see the whole picture before you make the pass, Hannah!'

I would have done that anyway, I thought, amused. I glanced up as I pushed forward into the opposition's half. Grace was free, but there were two defenders barrelling towards her.

'Quick, Hannah!' Dad yelled, 'Don't hang about – get the ball to Grace!'

I made a lightning decision. The other team were obviously terrified of Grace's shooting skills, and so they were concentrating their defending on *her*. They expected me to pass to her, too. Well, I wasn't going to! Guessing that Lauren would be streaking up alongside me in a second or two, I sent the ball forward into space.

Immediately Lauren's diminutive figure raced past me and pounced on the ball. The defenders were wrong-footed and had to chase desperately back over to our side of the field to try and stop her. But they were too late. Lauren pelted into the box and smashed the ball into the net.

'GOAL!' Georgie roared joyously, dancing up and down in our goal.

The rest of the team rushed over to Lauren and leapt on her. As I disentangled myself from the heap, I glanced over at my family. They were all applauding except Olivia, who just looked bored. Then Dad gave me a double thumbs-up and I smiled.

We won the match 3-1 with two more goals from Grace and Sally. I don't even know if Dad shouted at me again. I didn't notice because I was enjoying myself too much.

'Martha's Merry Men are the best!' Lauren announced as we danced our way into the changing-rooms after the game. 'That was *awesome*!'

'I totally agree,' said Freya, following us in. Martha was with her. 'You were fantastic and I can't wait to see you do all that again for our team next week!'

'These six have done well,' Martha remarked. 'Even though they've had their ups and downs, they've stuck at it and built a great bond between them.'

She grinned at us, and we all nearly fainted with shock.

'Wow, we *did* get her to smile – eventually!' Jasmin whispered, as Martha and Freya went out. 'She looked *almost* human!'

'Martha's right,' I said, pulling off my shirt. 'We're mates now, aren't we? And it's all because of this week.'

'Let's get together all the time, not just at training,' Grace suggested eagerly.

'And not only for football,' Jasmin added. 'Let's do silly *girlie* things too.'

'Yes, and maybe we won't argue so much now that we can yell *MILKSHAKE!* at each other!' Lauren pointed out.

That was enough to set us off laughing.

'*How* many bits of strawberry did we pick out of your hair, Jasmin?' Katy asked teasingly.

Chattering away, we got changed, said goodbye

to Martha and Mike and then went to the car park to meet our parents.

'Hannah, you were great!' Mum declared, giving me a hug. 'You were even better when you ignored what your dad said!'

'Thanks very much, Louise.' Dad rolled his eyes, but he was smiling.

'I'm proud of you, Hannah,' said Grandpa.

'Way to go, Hannah,' Olivia murmured lazily, pushing her sunglasses on top of her head. 'I can see I'm going to have to get used to living with a football-mad family. I might even get to like football myself, who knows?'

I stared at her, too surprised to say anything.

'Hannah, Carol's agreed that Olivia can move in with us for the foreseeable future,' Dad rushed to explain.

'Oh.'

I was shocked to find that I wasn't *quite* as upset about this as I would have been a few weeks ago. But there was a hint of a challenge in Olivia's eyes as we stared at each other. I realised then that the war between Olivia and me was far from over. In fact, it might even get worse. But I also realised that the reason why I wasn't so worried was because I was a much stronger person now. This time I *wasn't* going to allow Olivia to manipulate me and make me feel bad. A lot of it had been in my own head, anyway.

I glanced across the stadium. Lauren, Jasmin and Grace were just leaving with their families, and they all waved at me. Katy and Georgie were chatting to Freya and Georgie's dad, and they both smiled at me.

No, I didn't care so much about Olivia any more. Not when I had five fantastic new mates on my side.

THE BEAUTIFUL GAME

To WIN a **Nintendo DSI Console**
– and other spectacular prizes –
just answer the following questions:

1. What is the name of the football club
   that Hannah plays for?

2. What is Hannah's big secret?

3. How does Katy's watch get broken?

Log on to

www.thebeautifulgamebooks.co.uk

NOW for your chance to win!

THE BEAUTIFUL GAME

Can't get enough of Hannah and her friends?

Here's a taster of book 2 –
LAUREN'S BEST FRIEND

CHAPTER ONE

One minute I was running along with the ball at my feet. The next minute, I was rolling around on the grass, all the breath knocked out of me, clutching my sore ankle.

'Ouch!' I groaned, as the whistle blew. 'Ref, *do* something will you?'

'Oh, stop whining,' the Melfield United defender, Lily Scott, muttered as she walked away. 'I didn't hurt you *that* much.'

Well, maybe she didn't, but that wasn't the point, was it? It was about the *tenth* time she'd tackled me so clumsily during the game, and I'd had enough.

I'm a nice person usually, honest. But sometimes…
Well, I don't know what happens, but my blood
starts to boil and I get this red mist in front of my
eyes and I lose my temper in a big way and then
I just don't *care*.

Which was exactly how I was feeling right now.
Fuming, I jumped to my feet and raced after Lily.

'Lauren!' Jasmin shouted from behind me.
'*Milkshake*!'

I slowed down and glanced round. Jasmin,
Hannah and Grace were all running towards me,
screaming, '*Milkshake! Milkshake!*'

'Big, frothy, strawberry MILKSHAKE!' Katy
yelled at me from defence. Meanwhile Georgie, our
goalie, was jumping up and down in the box,
miming slurping milkshake through a straw.

The referee and the Melfield United players were
staring at us in bewilderment. Even the rest of our
team-mates were watching, open-mouthed, and so
were the groups of parents standing around on the
touchline. But I stopped dead and started giggling.
I guess you're probably thinking that our team, the
Springhill Stars, are as nutty as a bar of fruit and nut
chocolate by now! But we're not *really*.

I guess it all started when our coach Freya chose

the six of us – that's me, Jasmin, Grace, Hannah, Georgie and Katy – to go on an intensive football course during the Easter holidays. I didn't know the others that well before then, although Jasmin and I had been to the same primary school. Hannah and Katy were both new to the team, so I didn't know them at *all*. Anyway, during the week the course lasted, the six of us became mates. Ooh, that sounds so easy, doesn't it? Well, it wasn't! We had some mega ups and downs because we're all such big characters (and that's a nice way of putting it). We made up though, but then it all nearly fell to bits again because I played a silly joke on Hannah. I felt *so* bad about it afterwards, and I really thought that was *it*. The end of our friendship. But to cut a long story short, we decided to have our very own special word to say when we thought someone was getting angry and they ought to cool it. You've guessed it! *Milkshake!*

'OK, you mad, crazy people,' I said, holding up my hands. 'I give in.'

'It worked!' Jasmin squealed in delight. 'We're winning 2-1, Lauren, and you *mustn't* get sent off now.'

'You're a star.' Grace patted me on the back.

'Now just calm down and count to ten and *breathe*.'

'Lily's really giving you a hard time, Lauren,' Hannah chimed in. 'But you're doing brilliantly, and there's only five minutes left to go.'

'Sorry to interrupt,' the ref called grumpily, 'But can we finish the game, please?'

As Hannah ran to get the ball to take our free-kick, both Georgie and Katy gave me a double-thumbs-up from the other end of the pitch. I felt quite proud of myself. For once, I'd managed to control my hot temper, thanks to the other girls. But if Lily Scott hacked me down again, there was still every chance that I might just do something I'd regret the second after it happened!

I sighed as Hannah booted the ball to Grace. Whatever the others said, I'd had a rubbish game, and actually it wasn't just because of Lily Scott's terrible tackling. I was feeling all *bleurgh* at the moment, and I wasn't really sure why...

I suppose a bit of it was because we'd started back at school this week after the end of the Easter holidays. But I think it was mostly because the Stars had gone all out for promotion to the next league this year, but we hadn't made it. We only had four matches left until the end of the season, and we were completely out of the running. I was *so* disappointed. Oh, and Mum and I had gone to Florida last week on holiday, which had been a *total* disaster—

'Lauren!'

I jumped and realised, too late, that Emily Barnard had just passed the ball to me. Helplessly I watched it spin out of play for a throw-in to Melfield.

'Sorry,' I called back. Emily shrugged and rolled her eyes, looking a bit put out.

'You're half-asleep, Lauren,' Georgie called from our goalmouth. Grace is our captain, but Georgie likes to yell at us all the time. She says it keeps us on our toes. 'Wakey, wakey!'

Feeling guilty, I glanced over at Freya, who was standing on the touchline. She frowned at me, shook her head and tapped her watch. I knew what that look meant. *Only a few minutes to go – concentrate!!!*

'You need a kick up the backside, Lauren Bell,' I muttered to myself, 'and I'm giving you one right now!'

I was usually a bit disappointed whenever a match ended, especially when it was a sunny, blue-sky kind of morning like today, but I was very relieved to hear the final whistle. I'd managed not to make any more mistakes (basically because I'd only touched the ball once or twice during the last few minutes anyway), and we held on to our lead to win.

'Thanks for a good game, Lauren,' Lily Scott said, coming over to slap me on the back as the spectators applauded.

'You too, Lily,' I replied, resisting the overwhelming urge to kick her on both ankles.

'Ooh, I know exactly what you're thinking, Lauren,' Jasmin said, wagging her finger at me as Lily went off with the rest of her team-mates. 'You *so* mustn't do that!'

I grinned at Jasmin and slung my arm across her shoulders. 'OK, I'll be a good girl, I promise.'

'How long will *that* last, Lauren?' Grace teased. She pulled out her pink hair elastic and let her straight, shiny blonde hair cascade down over her shoulders.

'Grace, how do you always manage to look so gorgeous after a match?' Hannah asked enviously, coming to join us as we strolled off towards the changing-rooms. 'I just *know* my hair's sweaty and sticking up, and that my face is as red as a tomato.'

'Oh, but Lauren's the glamorous one at the

moment,' Grace added, smiling at me. 'Look at you, all brown and healthy after your fab holiday.'

I smiled back, but said nothing. I hadn't told the others just how *not* fab my holiday had been. Mum had spent most of the week on her phone and laptop, sorting out work problems. So we'd hardly used the pink limo she'd hired, and I'd spent most of the time sitting by the pool on my own. I'd got a great tan, but I was bored out of my *skull*. I'd probably gone a bit over the top, though, boasting to the other girls about the wonderful time I'd had. I don't know why. I guess I just didn't want them to feel sorry for me...

About the Author

Narinder Dhami lives in Cambridge with her husband Robert and their three cats, but was originally born in Wolverhampton. Her dad came over from India in 1954, and met and married her mum, who is English. Narinder always wanted to write, but after university taught in London for ten years before becoming a writer.

For the last thirteen years Narinder has been a full-time author. She has written over 100 children's books, as well as many short stories and articles for children's magazines. *Hannah's Secret* is the first book in The Beautiful Game series.

Since her childhood, Narinder has been a huge football fan.

Other Orchard books you might enjoy

The Shooting Star	Rose Impey	978 1 84362 560 5
My Scary Fairy Godmother	Rose Impey	978 1 84362 683 1
Hothouse Flower	Rose Impey	978 1 84616 215 2
Introducing Scarlett Lee	Rose Impey	978 1 84616 706 5*
Do Not Read This Book	Pat Moon	978 1 84121 435 1
Do Not Read Any Further	Pat Moon	978 1 84121 456 6
Do Not Read Or Else!	Pat Moon	978 1 84616 082 0
Pink Knickers Aren't Cool!	Jean Ure	978 1 84616 961 8
Girls Stick Together!	Jean Ure	978 1 84616 963 2
Girls Are Groovy!	Jean Ure	978 1 84616 962 5
Boys Are OK!	Jean Ure	978 1 84616 964 9

All prices at £4.99, apart from those marked * which are £5.99.
Orchard books are available from all good bookshops,
or can be ordered direct from the publisher:
Orchard Books, PO BOX 29, Douglas IM99 1BQ

Credit card orders please telephone 01624 836000 or fax 01624 837033
or visit our website: www.orchardbooks.co.uk or
email: bookshop@enterprise.net for details.

To order please quote title, author and ISBN and
your full name and address.

Cheques and postal orders should be made payable to 'Bookpost plc.'
Postage and packing is FREE within the UK
(overseas customers should add £1.00 per book).

Prices and availability are subject to change.